EDWARD KING

An Exorcist Possessed

by Rick Wood

There are two kinds of people.

Those who lie in the darkness and struggle against their demons.

Or those who turn on the light and kick some arse.

This book is dedicated to those who choose the latter.

"Don't let anyone deceive you in any way. For that day will not come unless the apostasy comes first and the man of lawlessness is revealed, the son of destruction."

2 Thessalonians 2:3

1

20 September 1984

Sixteen years before millennium

Eddie heavily desired to punch this kid square in the jaw.

He knew he shouldn't. Jenny had told him he shouldn't. His teacher had told him he shouldn't. Hell, even his disgrace of a mother had told him he shouldn't.

But he wanted to nonetheless.

He wanted to so, so much.

"Your sister's dead," Billy sang, his fat belly jiggling and his wide, merciless smirk spread across his chubby face. "Your sister's dead, haha!"

Jenny clutched onto Eddie's arm, pulling him away, doing everything she could to avoid him getting hurt.

"Come on, Eddie, just ignore it."

He couldn't just ignore it.

Not when that fat idiot, Billy, was talking about his deceased sister.

Eddie paused, darting between thoughts. He could go with Jenny and ignore Billy. Or, he could turn around and land his fist straight in this kid's mouth.

Eddie's dad did it all the time. He punched anyone he could find when he was angry.

Eddie's mum in particular seemed to annoy his dad. Eddie had seen it. Ever since Cassy had died, it was all the old man did – besides drink and moan.

But he hated him for it. He dreaded becoming like his dad. He dreaded becoming someone who took his aggression out on others.

"Eddie, please, come on."

He considered Jenny's distraught eyes. She cared for him. She was his family. He should listen to her.

Fine. I'll walk away.

Turning his back to the hefty little bastard, he allowed Jenny to grab his arm and drag him away.But he could feel the kid's smirk radiating against his back. Despite knowing Jenny was right, despite knowing it was the right thing to do, he felt sick letting Billy get away with it.

"Yeah, that's right. Let your bitch drag you away."

He froze.

Had he just called Jenny a bitch?

Jenny's eyes begged him to move. He couldn't. He was frantically immobile. Furiously still. Adamantly undecided.

"Just like you let your bitch sister die."

No.

Eddie spun around and pulled his arm out of Jenny's grasp. He charged toward the cocky, obese prick, who was standing there guffawing away.

Eddie was determined to shut his gob once and for all.

"You shut the hell up, you arsehole!"

A crowd had gathered. A crowd that was laughing at him. Laughing at Eddie.

Their sniggers and jeers made him shake with rage and he couldn't control it.

Eddie aimed his fist straight at Billy's fat face. But Billy was quicker than his appearance suggested and he dodged the blow, countering with one of his own that landed square in Eddie's stomach. Eddie doubled over, and Billy slammed a second punch into the back of his head. Eddie fell to the ground, vision blurring, shock skittering from the base of his skull and down his spine.

Hysterics surrounded him. The circle of mocking fits of laughter encompassed him in a sore, humiliated mind. It felt like every kid in the school was there, determined to celebrate his misery.

Billy had insulted Jenny. Billy had insulted Eddie's sister. And now, Billy had just knocked Eddie to the floor in front of the entire school.

Jenny was by his side in a flash, stroking back his hair and checking his bleeding nose.

"Oh my God, you're killing me!" Billy snorted, having to bend over from laughing so much.

"Why don't you just piss off!" Jenny venomously aimed at Billy.

A dramatic "ooh" resounded from the surrounding crowd.

"Just 'cause you're fat as fuck, doesn't mean you have to take it out on everyone else!" she continued, leaping to her feet. She stormed forward and squared up to him.

"Oh, you gonna fight me too?" Billy beamed. "This what it takes Ed'? Your slut doing your fightin' for ya?"

"I am not a slut!" she spat into his face, an inch away, her eyes livid. "And if you so much as harm one hair on his head, or even think about bothering him again, then yeah, I'll fight you. And I will destroy you, you fat bastard."

The laughs continued; not in aid of Jenny, but at her expense. A ridicule of her feeble attempt at sticking up for her best friend.

With a last glare at Billy, who still looked irritatingly smug, she turned back to Eddie, who still lay on the ground, blood dripping from his face. She put her arm around him and helped him to his feet. He fumbled forward dizzily, her arm the only thing keeping him steady.

"Don't worry, Eddie," she whispered in his ear. "We'll get you to the nurse. We'll tell the teacher."

"I don't want to tell the teacher."

"You've got to tell someone."

"Just help me to the bathroom, I'll be fine."

But this wasn't the end. Eddie could still hear Billy shouting in the background, continuing the vile, contemptuous insults.

Eddie daren't fight. He'd just be humiliated again.

Instead, he would limp away with his only friend and cry in the cubicle of the toilet. Cry over the words that wounded him, over the black eye he could feel throbbing.

Cry over the memory of his sister who had only died mere months ago.

He missed her so much.

"You wimp! You pussy!"

The words continued.

"Your sister was a bitch too, a pathetic little bitch!"

Eddie fell to his knees. Jenny rushed to his side, putting an arm around him, but he pushed it off.

The rage inside of him grew. It rose like a mouthful of sick, filling him, flooding through him like a tsunami of wrath.

He was not letting Billy talk about his sister like that.

Eddie could feel his veins pulsating, the blood coursing through them like the waves of a furious ocean. The anger rose within him, a volcano of hostility about to spew over.

He did not feel like himself. This was not him.

He was not in control.

He didn't know what this was, but he hadn't ever felt this before.

He felt powerful. Furious, but powerful.

As he climbed to his feet, the pain in his eye and his gut faded. The kid he detested continued to torment Eddie's.

"*Et succendam vos in inferno,*" Eddie growled.

Jenny stood back in horror. What did he just say?

What does that mean? I don't even know what that means... Eddie mused.

But he didn't care. He wasn't in charge, his anger was.

And it felt good.

"What's the matter bitch boy, you coming back for more?"

Eddie's eyes narrowed, his stare intensifying. Thunder grew within him. All he focussed on was this prick; this horrible, disgusting child he hated with all his might.

He was shaking uncontrollably, practically in a seizure.

"What's the matter, you –"

Billy halted mid-sentence.

Billy wretched.

Billy gagged.

With a jolt of Billy's body, his mouth opened and a sea of vomit came strewing out, lumps of blood and undigested fat soaring out of his mouth.

The crowd around him jumped back and dispersed in shock. They didn't want to be anywhere near this.

Then Jenny saw something. And, being honest, Jenny was never entirely sure whether she had seen it. She couldn't swear either way.

Just before Billy fell over, before he capsized flat out onto his face – she saw him lift inches of the ground. Only momentarily, for less than a second, before he was brought sailing back to earth by his face, his nose slamming into the cement with an audible crack that reverberated around the playground.

Dinner ladies were by Billy's side in an instant.

Eddie's anger left him. He had no idea what had happened, what he had just done.

"Eddie?" Jenny prompted him, her hand on his shoulder.

"Get me to the bathroom," he coughed, his pain abruptly returning. He wanted to be as far away as possible from the commotion occurring the other side of the playground.

Billy never picked on Eddie again. In fact, he went out of his way to avoid crossing paths with him.

And as Jenny stood beside Eddie, watching him clean himself up, washing pieces of stone out of his face, she couldn't help but stare. She had no idea how he had done what he had done. Or if he had actually done what Jenny thought she saw.

She just stared at her best friend. Stared with absent knowledge.

She never asked, never wanting to know the answer.

In time, the memory simply faded like Eddie's black eye.

2

6 December 2001

One year eleven months after the millennium

Jason Aslan's head pounded against the floor and his body fell limp.

Kelly – an innocent young woman, now possessed with the devil's hatred – looked down at his decapitated body with a satisfied grin.

On the other side of Jason's body, Eddie King was poised, mid-exorcism. Behind him, his mentor and friend, Derek, was frozen, as though unable to believe what he had witnessed.

Jason didn't know what happened next in the room.

He couldn't; he was dead.

He had no idea what reaction anybody had, how his wife was told, how his granddaughters reacted. Yes, if he passed on to heaven where he belonged, he would have found out. Should it have been his choice, he could have watched over them for all eternity.

But this wasn't an ordinary death. This wasn't just any murder. He didn't die because it was his time.

This murder was committed by Satan. The devil. Lucifer himself.

Unbeknownst to witnesses in the room; Eddie, Derek, and Kelly (even though she was absently trapped inside her body, secluded in a vacant space somewhere inside her own mind), he had been killed by this ruler of hell for a reason.

He was part of the plan. Part of the plan for the devil to lead his heir to his right-hand side, as the next in line as the ruler of hell.

Eddie faced the devil only days later. He had crossed over to hell to save Derek's soul, and he had retrieved it.

Eddie had won. Eddie had beaten the ruler of hell on the enemy's turf.

Eddie believed, as had anyone who knew of these events, that when he had avoided the devil taking Derek's soul, the fight was over. That the victory happened because the devil had lost. Eddie had succeeded somehow. Triumphant in his fight.

But could he really be so cocky as to believe he had beaten the devil? And in hell, where the devil ruled, nonetheless?

Little did Eddie know, this was also part of the plan. Part of the scheme the devil had concocted. Part of the twisted ruse.

The devil found it funny that Eddie would have the audacity to think he had won a battle against him. No one would ever win anything against him. He wasn't what caused nightmares – he *was* nightmares. He was what people had feared for thousands of years, and if it was part of his plan, it would be as good as fate.

Jason didn't know this. But he would.

"Wh – where am I?" Jason stuttered, opening his eyes to pitch-black, no sound around him. The faint odour of burning wafted past him and he could taste smoke.

The room he had died in was gone. Now he was somewhere else.

"Jason Aslan!" boomed a voice made up of many low pitches, ringing down his spine.

"Where am I?"

"It matters not where you are," smiled the voice. "You are nowhere, and everywhere. But seeing as your feeble human mind has to make sense of everything – I call this the purgatory."

"Purgatory…?" Jason echoed. He wiped his face, checked his arms, felt his legs. He was all there. Except, he wasn't. He could feel skin and bone with his hands, but not in his body. He was light, like air; weightless, painless. He did not breathe, but he felt breath. His heart did not beat, yet he could touch his chest with his hand and grip it firmly in his palm.

"Relax. You will have plenty of time to make sense of where you are. You will be here for a very long time."

"What? Why?" Jason was sure he could think of more pertinent questions, but the terrifying confusion of his mind couldn't make sense of anything past the alarm of being stuck in this complete darkness indefinitely.

"I have a task for you, Jason Aslan. You complete it, you will have your very own place in hell."

"In hell? I'm a good person!"

"A good person? Someone who has devoted their life to debunking those who attempt to oppose the devil? My child, you have done my work for me!"

Jason placed his hands on the ground, feeling a solid surface. He crawled forward, expecting to bump into something, for the path to end somewhere, but all he found was more darkness.

"I will use you as my eyes and ears. My representative. To communicate with my son and heir."

"I…" Jason was speechless. He understood nothing. It made no sense to him whatsoever.

"But until then, you will wait here. Until I call you."

"Where is here? What am I to do while I wait?"

But there was no answer. The presence he had felt had faded, and all that he felt was solace.

His mind turned to flashes of memory.

The exorcism.

That girl.

His neck. Snapping.

She… she chopped my head off. I'm – I'm dead…

As this dawned on him, he considered with frightening uncertainty what this meant. This was his consequence, his 'after' – his never-ending.

This was where he had been sent after a lifetime of denying the possibility. He would feel foolish, if he could feel such things in the hazy state of mind in which he resided.

"Is anyone there?"

He fell silent, listening for a response. Eventually, he would get used to the echoing silence.

3

27 April 1994

Five years, seven months before the millennium

Derek's trip down the coast of South Africa to Umtata had been unbearable. He was sweltering in the intense heat. The air was humid, and his clothes were wet with sweat. He couldn't stand it. He despised heat. People always complained about how cold his house was, but he liked it.

Despite the heat, Derek could feel an optimism within the air. The country was in high spirits, and rightly so. It was the morning of the election, and they were on the cusp of their first black president. Some man he had heard of who had been freed from an unfair, long-term stint in jail, by the name of Nelson Mandela. He knew little about the country, but there was a feeling in the air that change was on the horizon. A feeling of optimism that better times were to come.

All Derek could feel was a sickening feeling in the

pit of his stomach. He had been requested specifically for this exorcism by a man he had never heard of, who was sure that, despite his amateurish, sparse credentials, he had what it took. So much so, this man was willing to risk his wife's future on it.

Derek couldn't figure out who was the bigger fool – him for making this journey, or this man who had paid for the journey.

Derek felt perturbed, and rightly so, considering there was nothing visible in the distance but hills and green. The bus driver had halted his rickety old vehicle on the side of a dusty road and grunted at Derek. Now, trudging across one of said fields, he felt foolish that a slight feeling of intimidation toward this bus driver had meant he had been coerced onto a gravel road and left to watch as the bus sped away.

All he could see were fields either side of the gravel road he had been travelling down for miles. Taking his scrunched map out of his bag, he checked the location.

Mbolompo, Umtata.

He was there.

But where was there, exactly?

"Derek?" came the voice of a young boy with a thick South African accent. Derek spun around and laid his eyes upon a dangerously thin black child, who couldn't have been more than eleven years old.

"Yes?" Derek responded, rather timidly.

"This way," the boy demanded, and turned on his heel, not glancing back to see if Derek was keeping up. Derek sighed, thought *what the hell?* and shuffled along behind him.

Within minutes, the boy had led him to a large field, home of a community of around twenty wooden huts. They were like a cross between a hut and a caravan, bunched up together in a close group of no particular shape. The roofs were pointed into a circle, the structures inches from each other, with a fence surrounding the gathering of small, but homely, buildings.

The boy knocked on the door of one of these homes and a man walked out, with a smile spread across his face. This man looked like the happiest man Derek had ever seen. He had his arms spread wide, grinning at Derek, adorned in multi-coloured robes. Derek almost looked behind himself, he felt so unassured about why this man's overly happy greeting would be aimed at him.

"You must be Derek," the man practically sang, happily rejoicing at his new friend's presence. "It is lovely to meet you."

Derek fumbled his hand forward for a hand shake – but, before he knew it, he was being embraced in a large hug.

"I take it you met my son." The man gestured toward the boy who had hastily brought Derek here.

"I did, yes. Are you Bandile Thato?"

"I am."

"It's lovely to meet you, Mr Thato. Although to be honest, I'm not entirely sure why I am here."

"Come, let's have a drink. All will be explained."

*

Derek lifted a plastic cup of what might have been beer, if the colour wasn't that of muddied water. Either way, it was delicious, and he thoroughly enjoyed it.

"What is this?" he enquired.

"Umqombothi," Bandile replied, smiling across

the table at his most welcome guest.

"It's delicious. How is it made?"

"It is a beer, made from corn." He spoke with cheerful South African accent. "It is made by our women, for our men. I am most glad you enjoy it."

Derek slurped it once more, then placed the cup on the table, lifting his gaze to Bandile.

"I don't imagine you brought me here to taste your beer, Bandile," Derek prompted.

"No, I didn't."

"Can I ask, how did you hear about me? I'm not a recognized exorcist, I'm barely an amateur. I have attended only a handful... I just wonder how my name travelled across the world."

"I know your name because I must know your name."

"I – I don't understand."

"Your name came to me. I can't explain it any better than that."

Derek's head filled with confusion. He felt like Bandile had explained it clearly, yet not at all.

"My name came to you?"

"I can tell you many things, Derek," Bandile smiled, looking out the window at the sun setting on the horizon. "I can tell you that Nelson Mandela will win this presidency and he will begin his first term on 10th May this year."

"You can't possibly know that –"

"I can tell you that seven will die and fifty-two will be injured on 26th January, 1995, in India," he continued, not responding to Derek's scepticism. "I can tell you that, in 1999, three people will die in London in April. I could even tell you that in 2002, you will be instrumental in playing a part in the biggest threat known to man. You want to know how I know this?"

"Yes," Derek replied, leaning forward, intensely curious. "I do."

"Well, I cannot tell. Because I do not know. Same as I do not know why we are here. I do not know why you are the one who must save my wife. I do not know why you will manage – I. Just. Know."

Derek leant back, his head full of questions he found tough to verbalise.

"Does this come to you in visions? In dreams?"

"Sometimes. Sometimes it just comes to me in numbers. Sometimes it's in the corner of my eye, or in the corner of my mind. That is how I know you will be the one to rid the demon from my wife's body."

"Because… you saw it?"

Bandile gently nodded. His smile had fallen, his demeanour had slipped; like he was revealing the true burden that weighed upon his shoulders.

"I have written all I know down in a book of prophecies. I have only made three of these books. I do not wish to keep any of them."

"Why not?"

"It is not a blessing to know when people will die. It is a burden that I cannot do anything about. I must record it, I must let people know somehow. And, same as I know the sun will rise tomorrow, I know it is you who needs this book. It is you who needs to know what is in it. And I will give it to you, in return for you freeing my wife."

Derek couldn't believe it; this man knew more about him than he did. He had no idea about his future, where it was going, what he even wanted to do… Yet this man was telling him he had written it all down in this book?

"Why? Why do I need this book, Bandile?"

Bandile dropped his head and considered, taking a deep, long moment of contemplation, being careful before he placed his burden upon this young man's shoulders.

"Because you will end up being instrumental in a war you don't even know you're fighting yet."

4

15 July 2002

Two years seven months after the millennium

Kelly's body lifted bolt upright. Her torso was rigid like a plank. Her forehead fiercely perspired.

As she willed her panting to subside, she squinted at the dark, taking in her surroundings.

She was in bed.

Eddie was asleep next to her.

The clock read 4.16 a.m.

There was nothing else there. They were alone. Completely, utterly alone.

She climbed out of bed, pulling her dressing gown over her arms. Trudging to the bathroom, she rubbed her eyes, trying to shake her mental fuzziness off. Glancing at herself in the mirror, she splashed hot water over her face.

She looked herself in the eyes. She was there. Just her, nothing else.

She was fine.

Why do I need to keep telling myself that?

She took in a deep breath of air and let her anxiety go as she breathed it out – just as Derek had advised her. It helped her. It calmed her breathing, stopped her sweating.

So she did it again. In, and out. In, and out.

"More dreams?"

She jumped and abruptly spun around. Eddie leant against the doorframe, his bare chest over his pyjama trousers, his eyebrows raised with an expectant look.

Kelly nodded, opening the cabinet beside the mirror and fumbling out medication. Eddie stepped forward and took it out of her hand – gently, with forceful softness.

"You know these don't help," he whispered in her ear, quietly affectionate.

"I know, they just help me sleep, and if I could just sleep…"

"It's not the right way and you know it."

He placed the pills back in the cabinet, turned her toward him and engulfed her in his arms. He held her tightly, pressing her face lightly against his chest, giving her his warmth, letting her know he was there.

"I'm just sick of seeing them… The glimpses… What I did…"

"You didn't do it."

"Not with my mind." She looked up at him. "But with my hands…"

She had been free of possession, liberated from the ordeal, for over six months. She had remembered nothing in the weeks that followed. Nothing of what she had done whilst the devil had taken over her body.

That was, she hadn't remembered anything until the past few days.

It was all coming back to her; in glimpses, at inopportune moments. In her sleep, in her daydreams, in the eyes of strangers.

This time, she had seen animals. A peaceful dream turned to unconscionable torment.

Cattle. Sheep. A dog. On a farm.

She had watched as her mind projected images of her hands dragging the entrails of a bull.

Then she saw herself fucking it.

She saw herself inserting the dead bull inside of herself and fucking it as she ate its heart.

She gagged. It was vile. It was graphic, and it made her feel disgusted and degraded to have these visions of her committing such vile acts.

"What was it this time?" Eddie enquired, relaxing his voice.

Kelly shook her head.

No. She couldn't say it out loud. Not to him.

She loved him too much and just couldn't bear him judging her.

"I'm not going anywhere," he assured her. "You can tell me."

"I can't, Eddie."

"But I need to know."

That was the wrong thing to say, and she knew Eddie could tell that as soon as the words left his mouth. This was no longer about her, it was about him. About him fighting the evil within himself, his endeavour to learn more about his opponent. His war with the devil, who had stolen her body from her.

His determination to journey into the depths of what he was fighting was ever-present in his mind and she knew that, but it wasn't what she needed. She was not a pawn between him and the king of hell.

She was his girlfriend. And she was not going to let herself become anything less.

However unfair it was.

"I'm sorry." He bowed his head. "I know it's not about me – it's just, you're the closest thing I have to learning more about what I'm facing. It would really help."

She freed herself from his grasp and meandered aimlessly back into the bedroom, leaving him standing with his hands on his hips in the doorway of the bathroom. Was that meant to be an apology? It was pitiful. All he did was justify his personal reasons for dragging her deepest, darkest visions from her mind.

She opened the curtains and gazed upon the street below. They lived in a lovely house. It had been nearly a month now, mostly on his wage. She was still a student, she couldn't match his salary. If she was honest with herself, sometimes it made her feel like she owed him.

Before she could debate it any further in her mind, she felt his arms tucking around her waist. She closed her eyes and sunk into his embrace, feeling its comfort, letting its warmth spread through her.

"I am sorry. I mean it. I'll let it go. I know this isn't easy for you. I love you."

"I love you too."

Kelly said nothing else. That was all she needed.

She gave him a soft kiss on the cheek and returned to bed. She laid on her side, facing the wall, and he put his arms around her from behind. She enjoyed the warmth, but within minutes his breathing became heavier and he was asleep.

She stayed wide awake until the alarm went at 7.00 a.m.

5

16 July 2002

Martin couldn't believe his luck.

The heat of his best friend's basement wasn't the only thing making him sweat. Beneath his hormonal teenage body was Kristy, her long, blond hair spread out across the arm of the sofa, her hands rubbing themselves up and down his back, her mouth passionately gnawing at his.

He felt her tongue brush against his and it sent tingles down his spine. He tried it again, poking his tongue warily into her mouth, and she returned the gesture.

Sweat dripped down the cusp of his neck, his erection pressing itself against her hip, her bare leg lifting itself around his waist and thoughts of lust and sex and breasts and stuff filled his head until –

"Kristy, Maggie, your mum is here!" came the cockblocking voice of Simon's mum up the stairs of the basement,

"Aw, shit!" exclaimed Kristy, immediately ceasing her lip contact with Martin, frantically pushing him off and grabbing her sister, Maggie, from underneath

Simon on the sofa across the room. "We got to go."

Maggie was equally alarmed and, before Martin's eyes could even readjust, they were sprinting up the stairs.

"Wait!" Simon jumped up. "Can we at least have your number?"

"We'll give you our number," Maggie replied, "if either of you can remember our surname."

Martin smirked. Simon looked blankly at him. His mouth remained agape as he returned his desperate gaze to the two gorgeous girls exiting his room.

"We'll see you at school," Kirsty interjected, evidently the happier of the two. "Bye, Martin."

With that they were gone, and Martin sat back with a satisfied smile. Simon slumped onto the sofa next to him and interrupted his gaze with an inquisitive stare.

"What?" Martin grunted.

"Mate, she was a right cow."

"Yeah, that's why I was after Kristy, and I asked you to take her moody sister," he laughed. "She is angry as shit."

Martin turned to the fridge next to him and opened it, looking for a beer.

"Bruv, what you doin'?" demanded Simon.

"I wan' a beer."

"Mate, those are my dad's. He'll kick my arse if he sees us nicking his beers. You already had one."

"One? How'm I meant to get pissed off one?"

"You ain't. You wan' get pissed, you get your own beer."

Martin shut the fridge and leant his head back. His mind returned to daydreams of Kristy.

"Kristy is proper nice though, ain't she?"

"Yeah, mate, she's nice. Next time bring one with a sister who ain't a bitch."

"Whatever." Martin's joyful mood immediately ceased. He had been desperate to get into Kristy's pants for ages, and Simon was being a right dick about it. "Let's go down the offy and I'll nick us a pack o' Stella."

He stood and took a cigarette out of his bag, lighting it and pretending not to choke as he inhaled a small drag.

"Can't be arsed, mate," Simon replied. "Think I'm just gon' stick here and play COD. Wan' play?"

"Nah mate. I hate fuckin' video games."

"What fifteen-year-old hates video games?"

"I do."

"Whatever. You can't smoke that fag in the house, my mum'll kill you."

With a sigh, Martin picked up his bag and marched up the stairs.

Fuck Simon, man, he told himself. *I'll go nick some Stella on my own, take it down the park. See if Kristy can come out later.*

After leaving the house, he made his way down the street, avoiding eye contact with the surrounding houses.

Kids cycled back and forth, shouting obscenities at each other. Some guy was napping on a sofa on his lawn. A bunch of boys Martin recognized from school were loitering against the road sign.

He hated this street.

He put his hood up and retained his tunnel vision, striding forward without altering his course.

He glanced at his watch.

Aw fuck, I'm late.

He didn't want to go home, but his nagging conscience told him to. His mum needed him. Without him, she could be stuck in her bed, starving. Last time he left her too long she ended up peeing herself.

Joys of being a young carer.

He daydreamed that he was a millionaire. He and Kristy would walk down the street and people would marvel at them. They would drive around in limos, have servants who would wash their dishes and iron their clothes. Maybe he could be a footballer, or Kristy could become an actress.

As it was, he still had a bowl of dirty dishes at home with his name on it.

Sighing a hesitant sigh, he trudged home, wondering what excuse he could come up with to a mother who was too ill to understand.

6

The sun poised in the midday sky over a clear, blue horizon. The grave sat still, where it had always been, a few clear words engraved upon it:

Cassy King
Gone but not forgotten
1976 – 1984

"She'd have been twenty-six this year," Eddie acknowledged, taking Jenny's hand in his.

"Wow. Really, that old?"

"Yep. Yet somehow, she will always stay eight years old. In our mind and in…"

His thoughts trickled off. He had fought Balam on Millennium Night to free her soul. Her eight-year-old soul, that had been detained in hell for sixteen years.

Luckily, he had won.

Yet, he still didn't understand why a demon had chosen his sister. Sure, he was supposedly a man with evil inside of him, he could understand why a demon may have gone at him.

But surely, Cassy was innocent in all of this.

Was it to torment him? To show off?

To push him over the edge?

The feel of Jenny's hand in his comforted him. She

had been his best friend his whole life. Neither of them could remember a time when they hadn't been close.

When Cassy died, when he had to leave his abusive parents' house, when Jenny met Lacy, when Eddie attempted suicide, when he met Lamashtu, Balam's slave demon, when he had to send himself to hell to rescue Derek and face the devil himself... She had been there for him.

Each and every time, she had been there.

And do you know what's changed? he thought to himself. *Not a damn thing.*

"She'd have been an incredible woman," Jenny smiled.

"You can't know that."

"Of course I do. If her brother is anything to go by, then I don't doubt it one bit."

He sighed. He felt her arm nestle around him and he reciprocated the gesture. They hugged. The only person other than Kelly he would ever let get this close.

His mind was still preoccupied with thoughts that Cassy's death was his fault. He was the one riding his bike with her. He was the one going fast and she was the one copying her older brother. He had tried to stop her, but by then, it was too late. She had met that car face first as it turned the corner.

He wished she was still alive. By his side. He had so much to tell her.

"How's work going?" Jenny mused, as if trying to avoid the situation becoming too emotional.

"Oh, fine," Eddie answered, pretending it was normal to talk about work by the grave of one's dead sister. "Derek's still off. No idea where he's gone.

Somewhere far off to find some answers or something, I don't know."

"I'm sure he'll be back soon."

"What about you? How's Lacy doing at the hospital?"

"Oh, she's queen of the nurses, she rules the roost. But you know her. Always so calm, while I'm always a mess."

He smiled. It was true. Jenny was the anxious one and Lacy was the one who was always down to earth. Lacy never let her emotions get the better of her; always so cool and collected, so calm.

"How's Kelly? She sleeping any better?"

"No, not really. She still wakes up with the dreams. I don't really ask her about them. She doesn't want to talk about what…"

He trailed off. How was he supposed to say these things aloud? "Her nightmares are still occupied by when she possessed by the devil." Five years ago, just the idea of it would have been too farfetched for him to even entertain.

Despite all he had faced, he still couldn't quite verbalise some of the bizarre situations he had been in.

"Come on, let's head back," Eddie decided.

"You sure?" Jenny confirmed.

"Yeah," he nodded.

They turned around and strolled up the path, their arms remaining around each other.

Then Eddie froze.

He had seen something.

It must be a trick of the imagination. Surely.

Eddie spun around. Across the graveyard, beside a large row of bushes, there had been a figure.

A figure accompanied by a bright-white light.

But it wasn't there.

But it had been. He was sure of it.

"What is it?" Jenny asked, peering at the blank space where Eddie stared.

Eddie let go of Jenny's embrace and stepped forward.

"Cassy…?" he whispered.

"Eddie, you know that's not possible."

No. It wasn't.

Or was it?

He had seen hell. He had been to purgatory. He had fought demons. Surely the line between the world of the living and the world of the dead could be crossed. Maybe it had, maybe he had seen something, maybe…

Or, maybe it was a figment of his imagination.

A deep longing manifested by his sub-conscious.

"Yeah. You're right."

They walked back toward the car.

As they did, Eddie couldn't help stealing another quick glance over his shoulder.

7

Derek looked down at his map. This appeared to be the right place; it was just a thoroughly odd location for a meeting.

'*Sabratha wa Sorman.*'

Northwest Libya, at what Derek considered to be a spectacle. The Sabratha Theatre. An archaeological site he knew little about, but stood agape before nonetheless.

He was fascinated by archaeology, but his endeavours into the paranormal had left little time for him to explore such an interest; and, despite discovering this to be a World Heritage Site, he was a bit embarrassed to say he knew little of its history.

Before him were light-brown remains, steps of an amphitheatre leading up to a few grand pillars, arched in front of a seemingly sturdy wall. He wondered how long this wall would last before it was eroded; the colour looked less rock or stone, more soft rock and sand.

"Magnificent, isn't it?" came a voice from behind Derek that he had not heard in a long time. A smile stretched across his face as he stood, embracing the man with a large, warm acceptance.

"Bandile," he acknowledged. "It's good to see you."

Bandile looked just as he had in 1994, but older. His skin had grown a few more wrinkles and his hair had all but gone, but he still had a strong physique, and a caring, warm grin.

"And it is lovely to see you, too, Derek. Come, let's walk."

They had a leisurely saunter, sharing a few moments of silence as they circled the grand architecture. Derek mulled over questions in his mind; he had so many, and wasn't sure where he should start.

"How is your wife?" he decided would be a good question to begin, especially considering his first full exorcism had been ridding a demon from her.

"Oh, she died a year or so ago."

"I'm sorry."

"Don't be. Her life was full, filled with happiness and love. However short, how many people can honestly say that?"

Derek loved the way Bandile talked about life. Even in Bandile's letters, he came across as concisely philosophical, with deep wisdom.

"So why on earth did you make me travel all the way to Libya to meet?"

"I can feel conflict on the horizon. I am needed here. My children are grown up, my wife is gone; they do not need me in Umtata anymore."

"How do you know there is conflict coming?"

"It is in my bones. Though it doesn't feel close… It is hard to describe."

Bandile came to one of the steps and settled himself down, gazing up at the sunlit sky. Derek sat next to him. The air was peaceful and calm, the sun was bright; it was hard to think of a sight such as this being a home to hate.

"So, you want to know about the book?" Bandile looked to Derek, straight to the point. He smiled, though it wasn't the large, warm smile he had given Derek upon greeting him; but a consigned, reluctant smile.

"Yes. There was a prediction in it, and... Well, it appears to be coming true."

"There are many predications in that book that have come true. That's why I passed the burden onto you."

"And now, Bandile, I need to bring it back. I need your guidance. I need to know what you see in the future."

Bandile took a deep breath in, held it, then slowly released it. His eyes fluttered and he dropped his head. Derek could see Bandile's conflicting thoughts; hesitance over thoughts Bandile couldn't articulate.

"You know what I say," he reminded Derek. "These things don't come to me in fully formed stories. They are glimpses. Images. Feelings"

"But the prophecy was rather clear, Bandile. It said the son of the devil would rise at the millennium. It said he would have no choice but to embrace the evil of his powers."

"And you believe you have found this man?"

"I believe so. I just don't know what to do."

"Run." Bandile's eyes widened and his voice faded to a worried tone Derek had never detected in him before. "He brings the very depths of hell with him. Run, leave him. He is evil."

"Except," Derek sighed, "he is not. I taught him to hone his powers. I taught him to use them for good. But now… the devil wants them back."

"This man, he is your friend, yes?"

"A very good friend."

"Kill him."

Derek's eyes dropped. He was stumped. His feelings spun with shocked, argumentative responses. This was an extreme solution he hadn't thought would be suggested.

"You come here hoping for a miracle. I cannot give you one. If you want to save your friend, and the world, from an eternity of pain – you need to end his life."

"I can't kill him, he is my friend."

"It would be mercy. Life is but a brief holiday from death. Release him."

Derek vehemently shook his head.

"Is there no other way?"

Bandile closed his eyes. He couldn't return Derek's apprehensive gaze.

"I will tell you what I have seen, what I have felt. I have seen fire, shooting from the sky. I have seen torture of innocent people. I have felt eternal pain, souls screaming out. I wish I hadn't, Derek, but this is what I have seen."

"You're wrong."

Bandile didn't reply. Derek knew denial was a common, but useless, response. It doesn't help anyone.

Bandile had never been wrong.

Derek stood. He put his hands in his pockets. His body reflected his mind; unsure, uncomfortable, wary.

Terrified.

"There has to be another way, Bandile. Please." Bandile stood and placed a warm hand on Derek's shoulder.

"Do you trust me?"

"What?"

"Do you *trust* me?"

Derek nodded.

"Then you will come with me, yes? I will give you what guidance I have, but I have to show you, yes?"

"Okay. Okay, Bandile. Where do we need to go?"

"The Killing Fields."

Derek winced. *What killing fields*?

"We will visit the skulls of Cambodia."

8

"So as you can see," Eddie continued, pointing toward his PowerPoint presentation, "his eyes are fully dilated."

He clicked along to the next slide where a close-up picture of a boy filled the screen. The boy's pupils were entirely black, his skin pale, and veins were sticking out prominently on his forehead.

"This was him as we began the exorcism. Tomorrow, we will look at the case study in detail." Eddie checked his watch. "And that is me running over. Thank you, folks. Have a good day."

As he exited the presentation and began logging off, the lecture theatre full of students filled with conversation as they all made their way down the aisles. Eddie looked up at a few of them, but avoided eye contact. This course had grown in popularity due to Derek, and he was feeling like he wasn't doing as good a job as the man they'd signed up to listen to.

As this thought crossed his mind, as if on cue, a young lady approached Eddie.

"Edward? I mean, Doctor King?"

"Yes," he peered at her, trying to recall her name, "Erm… Janet?"

"Close. Laney."

Eddie laughed politely.

"Laney. How can I help you?"

"I was just wondering when Doctor Lansdale was going to be back."

Eddie hesitated. He'd love to know the answer to that question himself.

"I'd love to tell you, but I can't. As soon as I hear anything, I'll let you know."

Laney smiled and walked away. She opened the door as Kelly entered, and turned to look back at Eddie for a moment.

"Oh, and Doctor King?"

"Yeah?"

"I think you're doing a great job in his absence."

Eddie couldn't help but smile. He needed to hear that.

"Thank you, Laney."

The door closed and Kelly approached Eddie with her eyebrows playfully risen.

"Got yourself a fan?"

"It's good to hear. These kids didn't come to hear me, they came to hear Derek."

Kelly tucked her arms around Eddie's waist and jokingly stuck out her bottom lip. She kissed him, softly and tenderly. He couldn't understand how she did that; with just a touch of her lips, she made the whole world seem trivial, like it was just her and him. Like she hadn't been possessed by the devil who, in turn, had tried to make Eddie fulfil his fate by becoming his successor. But the memory hit him smack in the middle of his head as soon as the kiss ended, and he was despondent again.

Giving Kelly a loving stroke of the hair, he removed himself from her embrace and removed his memory stick from the computer. He paused, gazing at the memory stick, playing with it in his hands.

"What is it?" Kelly asked, perching down on the side of a desk, watching him intently.

"I need him back Kel', I – I don't know."

"Why? You can do this without him. It's you who has this gift remember?"

Eddie scoffed. "Gift?"

"Well… you know what I mean."

"I may be the one who has it, but Derek is the one who knew what it meant way before I did. I mean, I understand why he had to go, why he's on his – 'voyage' – or whatever."

"Well there you go, then."

"But no, it's not right. I need to know what's next for me. I need to know if I'm going to end up ruling hell."

Kelly stood up and stepped toward him slowly. She placed her hands on the side of his face, stroking him gently, staring avidly into his eyes. She smiled sweetly, calming his nerves in an instant.

"You saved me," she reminded him, her voice soft and her tone comforting. "And you saved me from the devil himself. The one you're so scared of. I'm here, because of you."

"It's not all that simple though, is it?"

"Yes. It is."

"It's naïve to think we won. That this isn't part of some bigger scheme. It doesn't feel like it's over."

She leant her head against his, pulling him closer. He could smell her; not just her perfume, but her. It comforted him and excited him at the same time. It calmed his breathing yet quickened his heart. It was a manic tranquillity, like lucid adrenaline that filled his body with love he couldn't fight.

"Maybe it's not. But he's not here now. And Derek is trying his best to find out what to do. So you may as well just come with me, get a coffee, and have some lunch."

She was right.

Damn, she was always right.

She was young, but wise, sensible. He couldn't do anything about it at that moment. As much as he would like to, the best thing he could do was to just live day to day. Wait for Derek to do whatever he needed to do.

When the fight comes, it would come.

And Eddie could almost convince himself of that, until he remembered what exactly was at stake.

This world, everything on it, everything good.

Everything he was.

Or hoped he was.

9

The smell of urine hit Martin like a brick in the face.

He dumped his bag by the side of the door and solemnly pushed it closed behind him. Below his feet were a collection of envelopes, collecting into messy stacks. He kicked them to the side and plodded toward the stairs.

"Ma?" he called.

No answer.

In the kitchen, he saw a movement of light. He walked toward it. This is where he found his mother, Anna, hunched over in her wheelchair, vigorously shivering.

Martin pulled the blanket off the floor and positioned it around his mother. She snarled up at him with a face full of delicate fury.

"Where were you?" she haggardly barked.

"I was out, Ma."

"Where? I's eight o'clock. I've been waiting."

Martin had no answer. He should have been home, he should have sorted her dinner, he should have helped her into her bed; noticing the smell and a dried stain on her trousers, he guessed he should have helped her to the toilet as well.

But it wasn't fair.

Why should this be his responsibility? None of his

other mates had to deal with this crap. None of his mates had to pull their mum around the house, assisting her with every bloody thing because she's too bloody unable to move.

Why should he have to?

Just as soon as that thought took hold of him, guilt replaced it. It wasn't her fault she was this way. It wasn't her fault she'd had an accident. It wasn't her fault his dad left. It wasn't her fault that this stupid responsibility fell at his feet.

Still don't make it no fairer.

"Okay, Ma," he sighed despondently. "What do you want first? Toilet?"

"Well as you can see, I got too desperate for that!" Her nose scrunched up. He couldn't help thinking about how she looked like an angry rat; so small, helpless, and rodent-like. Yet, at the same time, scary enough to send most people running.

"I'll get some clean trousers and sort yuh soup," he concluded.

Only his mother ever spoke to him like that. A boy at school once tried it, told him he was a prick. Martin had planted his fist so hard into that lad's face he was suspended for a week; which had made no sense to him, as it meant a week off school, and he jumped at the opportunity for a week off. He'd just be skiving anyway.

Martin grabbed a pair of tracksuit bottoms from the washing basket and took them to her. He put his arm around her as she put hers around him, holding tight. With his spare hand, he pulled down her stained trousers, threw them in the basket, and helped her struggle into the other joggers.

It wasn't easy. She was gripping onto him, shaking

both out of illness and out of fear that she would fall.

As she sat back down in her wheelchair, he made his way to the kitchen cupboard, taking out an expired tin of soup. He looked over what else there was, but found no alternative. Checking that it was only a month gone, he poured it into a pan and waited for it to boil.

He turned back and looked at his mum, whose head was now facing away from him. He remembered the mum he was so close to as a child. A mum who would take him to the park, run around with him, lay on the beach with his dad as he played in the sea. A woman so full of life, so strong. She was his hero. Everything about her was full of love and he adored her.

Now look at her, he shook his head to himself. He knew he shouldn't think it, and he would always love her and take care of her regardless; but he envied other people's lives.

The lives of others whose disabled mother wasn't so close to death.

10

Jason's eyes groggily opened. He didn't know why he bothered opening them, there was never anything there. Just blackness. Repetitive absence torturing his mind.

He had no idea how long he had been stuck there, wherever it was. But time had dragged and his mind was going crazy. There was nowhere for him to go, nothing for him to do, no way he could entertain his wandering thoughts. It was so long since he'd seen light and he was beginning to forget what it was like.

"Grandpa?"

His head jerked up at the sound of a young, delicate voice, so distantly familiar his blood started racing. Except that it didn't. His blood didn't do anything.

Jason had no blood.

Finally, he saw a spark of light, a glimpse of whiteness before him, silhouetting a figure. He could make out the small size of the figure approaching, and a dress – it was definitely a dress. It blew in the wind, which confused Jason, as he felt no breeze.

"Grandpa?" repeated the child's voice.

Jason hazily lifted out his hands in hope, clasping for the child who steadily came into view. His absent heart melted at the sight of his five-year-old granddaughter, Ava.

"Ava!" he cried out, his voice croaky yet jubilant, unused. He clambered to his knees and stumbled forward, embracing her tightly in his arms.

She did not move. She did not react, she did not speak, nor even change her gaze.

He didn't care. He held onto her like he would never let go.

Then it hit him. He was dead, wasn't he?

He kept his hands gripped on her arms, afraid to let go.

"But if you're here…?"

"This is hell, Granddad," she replied, smiling. "We're all dead, here."

"But how? When?"

She wriggled free of his grasp and skipped away. She playfully flumped onto the floor.

The surroundings had changed. They were Jason's study.

He looked around, frantically searching for answers in the room that was identical to where he once lived.

Ava giggled and climbed underneath the desk.

"The devil can influence many people on Earth," she told him. "He sent a man for me. You should never be lonely here."

"What man?"

She said nothing.

"Ava, what man?"

"A bad man."

"What did he do to you?"

"He told me not to tell you. He says that if you do a…" she stumbled over the words, as if trying to recall something unfamiliar. "A sacred duty, then he will let us go to heaven together. Wouldn't that be nice?"

Jason edged toward her.

She wore the face of Ava. She spoke the voice of Ava. She even played like Ava.

But she didn't feel like Ava.

"And what if I don't?" offered Jason.

Ava stood and withdrew a lollipop, spiritedly putting it into her mouth.

Ava hated lollipops.

"He says that if you don't..." she turned serious, "Then bad things will happen to me, Harper, Mommy, and Nanny. He says that we will burn in hell for all eternity."

Jason fell to his knees. His face broke, his eyes welled up. He couldn't take this anymore. To have had what felt like an eternity of blank space surrounding him, then to be faced with this; it was beyond torture.

"You don't want to let us burn in hell, do you?"

He buried his head in his hands and wept. All the love he felt for this girl, the unaltered, complete, unshakeable adoration; they were using it.

And it was working.

"He says you need to answer," she commanded, bearing down upon him.

"Who is 'he'?" Jason uttered through stranded sobs.

"The same 'he' who put you here, silly. The same 'he' that has given you this sacred duty."

He choked upon hearing her call him 'silly.' It was a word Ava used all the time, any time he played with her, any time he pretended to pinch her nose or that he couldn't see her.

"Come on, Granddad. You don't want us to burn, do you?"

"Don't call me that!"

He clambered to his feet, falling forward at first, eventually finding his balance. He stood up tall, straightening his posture, dusting himself off, looking around him at the everlasting blackness that circled him.

The office had gone. In its place was the continual absence he had found himself stranded in before. Just him and Ava, facing each other in this never-ending pit of desolation. His gut wrenched, his heart burst, his fists clenched tightly.

"Why don't you come face me yourself!" he screamed out. "Why don't you show me your face?"

"He can't hear you."

Jason bowed his head. He moaned. He missed Ava so much, just as he missed his other granddaughter, Mia, his daughter, Harper, his wife, Linda. He had spent so long picturing their faces, and to see one of them once more, and for it not to really be her – it hurt. This was agony.

"Fine, I'll do it," he whimpered. "Just so long as you never show me this face again."

"So be it."

Breathing in deeply, he looked her in the eyes.

"What do you want me to do?"

11

Derek was in awe.

He had been vaguely aware of what terrible actions had led to the Skulls of Cambodia, but to be stood in front of the wall made from human skulls was indescribable. His jaw dropped and, neither he nor Bandile spoke for a while.

Some were white, some were grey; some were even brown. They were in poorly attempted rows, randomly positioned, in a complete dissonance to one another. Not that Derek would imagine someone creating a wall of human heads would consider positioning or symmetry.

"It's amazing, isn't it?" Bandile observed.

"Why would they choose to keep such a vile thing?"

"It is important not only to remember the good times, but the bad times. You should not deny your history." He turned to Derek. "If you were to deny your past rather than confront it, would you not be in danger of repeating the exact same thing?"

Derek's eyes didn't stray from the destitute

remains. Large, vacant eye sockets stared back at him, the top layer of teeth snarling from various angles. Death piled upon death. A reminder upon reminder of dark days past.

"I've heard about the killing fields," Derek acknowledged. "But I never… Why are we here?"

Bandile smiled.

"A quarter of these people's population were slaughtered in this genocide." Bandile spoke slowly and calmly. "From 1975 to 1979, people were executed not only for connections with a former government, but for being an 'intellectual.' For having an education. Wearing glasses even. Not only did a person give the orders for this act, masses of people carried them out."

"People sometimes do horrible stuff."

"Calling someone an insulting word is horrible, Derek. Punching someone for offending you is horrible. Arguing with your wife is horrible. This is not what humans are capable of through human acts alone."

"What are you saying?"

Bandile gestured toward a stone bench that was propped against a wall a few steps away. Slowly, they made their way over, Derek staring intently at Bandile, who gathered his thoughts. They sat next to each other, Bandile allowing a calm moment of contemplation to rest between them before meeting Derek's gaze.

"Acts like this are committed by humans, but people alone cannot commit such atrocities. Each and every one of these acts of terror have a hand from the devil."

"So, what, every genocide that's ever been done is

the devil's work? The Holocaust? The Crusades? The Killing Fields?"

"It's not the devil's work, it is people's work. But people cannot commit these acts of suffering alone. The devil just acts as a catalyst."

Derek turned from Bandile to the skulls and back again. The idea that the devil gave people the nudge they needed to commit such horrific acts was an unrealistic truth. It felt like an excuse, allowing mankind to remove the burden of guilt.

But it also made sense, in a way Derek found hard to admit to himself.

"So why are we here?" Derek concluded his thoughts, wanting to bring them back to the prophecy.

"When the devil lends his hand in such acts, he leaves an echo. His presence was here only decades ago, and that trace still lingers. We can use it."

Bandile put his hand on Derek's shoulder and looked him intently in the eyes.

"Derek, do you trust me?"

"Of course."

"Then the best chance you have is to take my hand and look into what remains. Trace his path with me, and you will be able to hypothesise his intentions."

Derek forced a vacant nod, his eyes remaining wide open and his expression unaltered. The idea of seeing through Bandile's eyes terrified him. He was so afraid of the future, having denied it for so long, he worried that even a glimpse might scar him.

"I – I can't…" he stuttered, shaking his head with a tremble. "I can't do what you do."

"Derek. I asked you if you trust me."

He placed his open palm out to Derek, awaiting Derek's hand in return. Derek had no idea what he would see, but he trusted Bandile. Bandile had guided him well so far. If it weren't for him, Derek wouldn't even be aware of the prophecy.

Which, in a way, would have made life all that much simpler.

"Derek?"

Derek knew he was going to have to do it. Suck it up. Be a man. This wasn't child's play anymore, not some silly exorcism with some silly demon on a silly kid. This was the real world. And he was about to land smack bang into the middle of it.

Clamping his eyes shut, he put his hand in Bandile's, who gripped tightly.

The wall disappeared. Everything shot past into blurs, like they were firing forward at a million miles per hour; yet Derek felt no movement in himself, no wind passing, no reaction from the elements.

The world passing him by at superior speed halted. He was in his office.

Eddie was there. Derek was looking at Eddie, who had his back to him.

Eddie was wounded. He was hunched over, his posture terrible, with his hand lifted to his mouth. A vile sound of demented sucking emulated from him, something dripping on the floor before him.

"Eddie?" Derek offered out into the room.

Eddie froze.

The sound ceased. Eddie did not move an inch. He remained huddled over.

Still.

Empty.

"Eddie, what are you doing?"

A deep-pitched groan crackled out of Eddie. It was the kind of groan Derek was used to from a demon possessing its victim. Maybe Eddie was host to something? Maybe Eddie was trying to tell Derek something? What was it?

"Eddie, what is going on?"

"I…" croaked Eddie, again in a low pitch and a crackled static in his voice.

"Eddie?" Derek edged a step closer. As he did, the stench of decay hit him, accompanied by the deep breaths of Eddie's sizzling throat.

"I… am not…"

Derek took another step closer, enough that he could touch Eddie. He held his hand out, but hovered it over Eddie's back, afraid to make contact.

"Am not what Eddie?"

"I… am not… Eddie…"

With a shot, Eddie spun around and Derek fell onto his back.

Eddie's face was an ocean of grey, blackness consuming his pupils and trickling down his face, dark red smeared over his lips.

"Eddie is not alone…" sang out the peculiar voice from Eddie's lips.

Derek's eyes shot open. He was on the floor in front of the skulls, Bandile standing over him, shouting at him to calm down. Derek' eyes abruptly readjusted and he saw that he had returned to Cambodia.

"Bandile!" he gasped.

Bandile nodded, waiting for Derek to say it.

"Eddie," he whispered. "He went to hell to get me, and…"

"Yes?"

"He… he came back wrong."

12

Kelly's eyes shot open. Sweat drenched her forehead, leaving a damp mark on the cushion beneath her. She had only intended to lie down for a short afternoon nap, and had awoken on the sofa from another nightmare.

It was the same situation. Another memory coming back to her, another nightmare she wished her mind had concealed. She wished the memories weren't real, but they felt far too lucid to be anything but.

She felt the animals' entrails plunging through her fingers into a heap on the floor. She smelled the foul odour of the death surrounding her; pigs, cows, sheep, in piles of reeking, rotten repulsion. She felt their thick blood dripping down her naked breasts.

But what made her gag most was the memory of the cautious movement she made over the animals, a hard feeling poking inside of her, the sight of a blood-drenched dead head beneath her as she cackled in rhythm to penetrations.

The recollection was too much. She darted to the bathroom and only just managed to lift the toilet seat before she projectile vomited thick, lumpy blood. The smell reminded her of the odour of rotten animals, and the feelings returned once more.

She was sick again.

Remaining poised over the toilet bowl, she willed the thoughts out of her mind. She forcibly numbed her memory, begging the repulsion to return to the back of her mind.

After around ten minutes, she flushed the toilet and stumbled to her knees. Using the wall to keep her upright, she fumbled her way to the kitchen and filled a pint glass with cold tap water. She gulped it down in one and returned the glass to the tap, filling it and downing it once more.

She felt her stomach. The queasiness had still not dissipated. She fumbled to the garden and knelt on the grass. Relishing the oxygen, she took continual intakes of breath, feeling the air freshening her lungs, rejuvenating her body.

Allowing her knees to give way, she dropped to her back and looked up at the sky. Clouds floated past in small puffs of white, the blue of the sky thick and the sun shining brightly.

She wondered where Eddie was. He was so good when it came to helping her when she felt like this. No expertly educated post-traumatic stress disorder therapist could help her in the way he could. As much expertise as a therapist carried, they wouldn't have the knowledge of her situation in the way Eddie did.

He had been to hell and back. Literally. Three times.

He had fought the devil in the depths of hell itself.

He had let Balam, one of the princes of the underworld, take his body so he could fight him internally and free his sister's soul of his claws.

He understood. And she needed him. Now.

She sat up, pausing as musky blurs floated in front of her eyes, a shaking dizziness rushing to her head.

These feelings kept coming back in waves of attacks, reminding her of what she had done when she had shared her body with the worst entity to have ever faced humanity.

She sniffed. She thought it was just her memory, but it wasn't; the smell of rotting decay lingered nearby. As she made her way to her feet, she followed it.

It drew her closer to the shed.

It grew stronger. It was foul, sickening, and it made her gag once more.

She placed her hand on the handle to the shed and slowly creaked it open, peering inside. It was too dark to see, but from the strength of the stench she knew this was where it was coming from.

Kelly fell to her knees. She retched. She was sickened, indignantly despairing with disgust.

A cat's head. Attached to the wall of the shed with a single nail. Ripped apart bloody entrails hanging from its open neck. No body attached or in sight.

Behind it was writing. Kelly recognised it, though she couldn't translate it. It was Latin. She had written it all over the walls when she was possessed.

She stumbled backwards against the wall of the house, wrapping her hands over her mouth as she coughed, willing her gagging reflex to go away. She stood far enough back that she could read the writing without having the smell the detestable stink.

Surge, diabolum

She had no idea what it meant. She patted herself down for a pen and found one in her back pocket. Squinting against the afternoon sun, she jotted that

Latin down on the back of her hand.

Did I do this? she wondered. *I can't have done…*

Once she had gotten over the initial shock and forced rationalisation back to her mind, she concluded she couldn't have done it. She and Eddie had moved into this house a month previous. It was around ten months ago that the entity was removed from her. She was no longer capable.

But if she hadn't written it, who had?

Knowing she was no closer to answering that question than she was to translating it, she made her way back into the house and into the living room. Eddie had a book-case full of books about the occult, exorcisms, and all that stuff. She was sure she had seen a Latin to English dictionary.

She traced her finger along the rows of books and, sure enough, there it was, on the third row down. She withdrew it and searched the first word.

Surge.

She found the correct page and used her finger to trace down the various words. Once she saw the word, she whispered the translation aloud.

"Rise."

She shuffled the pages to *D* and made her way through to the page, running down words beginning with Di until she found the word she was looking for.

"Devil."

The book dropped from her hands, clattering against the floor in a silent echo.

Someone had attached a cat's head, with a nail, to the wall of their shed, with the words written in Latin, with blood:

'*Rise, devil.*'

A single tear bled from her eye as she slumped against the wall. The wish that her ordeals were over faded like sun giving way to night.

What would happen to her if he rose again?

She buried her head in her hands and didn't move until Eddie returned home.

13

Derek's feet couldn't move fast enough through the airport. No matter how much he scuffled quickly forwards, Bandile always seemed to be keeping pace beside him with leisurely strides.

Once Derek had stood in line at the ticket queue, all the time tapping his wallet against his leg with agitation, and had urgently bought his ticket with thorough impatience toward the woman serving him, he stood with Bandile by the terminal.

They had ten minutes to wait until Derek's terminal opened, and to Derek it felt like ten years.

Questions shot through his thoughts and paraded around his mind: *Does Eddie know? What will he do? What is it that's come back with him? Is it even him?*

Seeing the terror etched over his face, Bandile placed a comforting hand on his shoulder

"Calm down, Derek," Bandile spoke, his peaceful, South African accent providing comfort. "There is nothing you will change by worrying."

"I just don't understand. Is it Eddie that has come back?"

"Why don't you ask me to explain it?"

"You mean – you know? You understand what is going on?"

"When we experience a flash such as we had in

Cambodia, my trained eyes see more than yours. I saw into Eddie's soul. I saw what is inside of him."

Bandile took a few small floating steps to a seat and sat down, gesturing toward the seat next to him. Derek's open jaw and narrowed eyebrows were frozen still. His perplexity had left him rooted to the spot. He shook himself out of his transfixion and took a seat next to Bandile.

"Where would you like me to start?" Bandile leant toward Derek, his chin propped on his hand. For the first time, Derek felt frustrated by Bandile's calmness, though knew it was probably better than panicking.

"Is it still Eddie?"

"It is still Eddie. But with a bit of the devil."

"How?"

Bandile momentarily shifted as he gathered his thoughts.

"You say he came to hell to rescue you?" He awaited Derek's nod of confirmation, then continued. "Well, the devil is not a fool, he is a powerful god, whether we admit it or not. He did this for a reason. I believe this reason – it was to latch onto him. Put a piece of the devil inside of Eddie so that he could return with it."

"But why?"

"To give Eddie a push. A prod – toward his destiny."

Derek rubbed his hand through his hair. This wasn't getting any better.

"Well then, how come he can't tell? When we see a person who has part of a demon latched onto them, they suffer. Usually they are aware of it on some level."

"Because he already has the devil in him. His fate means the blood of hell's legacy has been flowing through his veins since he was born. He will not notice any difference. He is already the product of the devil."

Derek leant his head back and closed his eyes. He wished he could just force it all away, bury his head in the sand, pretend it wasn't real. In the beginning, it had been oh so simple; he submitted a thesis, got his PhD, was given the opportunity to do his research and teach students.

How had it come to this?

"So what will happen to Eddie?"

"He will do things." Bandile stroked his chin. "He will do things that are… unusual. He is consciously unaware. He will do them without even registering, and he will not understand why or acknowledge what he has done."

"What kind of things?"

Bandile's warm smile turned to a sympathetic smile.

"Bandile, what kind of things? What will he do?"

Just at that moment, a voice echoed through the speaker: "Terminal five for London Heathrow is now open."

Derek didn't move. He didn't remove his unfaltering focus from Bandile's eyes. It was a difficult conversation, Derek knew that; but he was not the kind of person who appreciated being protected. He needed to know.

Yet there was still a piece of him wishing Bandile would not answer his question.

"Bandile, what is Eddie capable of?"

"It is not Eddie that is capable of it. It is the side of

him that has been lying dormant all these years, and is starting only now to come to the forefront."

"I get it, Bandile, I just need to know – are his friends in danger? Will he… hurt them?"

Bandile considered Derek's eyes and Derek looked back. Derek had never seen panic, complacency, or anger in Bandile's eyes. Bandile was always so calm, so wise, and knew what words he needed to impart on Derek at what time and why.

But in that moment, Derek willed Bandile to show a negative emotion. Something to show that the urgency and dread Derek was overcome with was present in Bandile as well.

Eddie was Derek's best friend. He had guided him to becoming the powerful exorcist the world had known. But in doing so, Derek was also responsible for awakening this side of Eddie; and whatever the consequences, he felt guilty for them.

Bandile said nothing. He stood. Derek followed, still staring, still awaiting an answer.

Bandile offered his open palm to Derek, who took it warmly. Their hand shake remained still, present and motionless in a moment of mutual reluctance.

"Come with me, Bandile."

"No, Derek. It is not my time."

Derek let go of his hand and picked up his bag, carrying it toward the terminal gate. He turned and looked toward Bandile who, for the first time, had a very slight etching of hesitancy over his face.

As they shared a moment of eye contact, communicating their worry without words, Derek mulled over what Bandile had just said.

"It's not my time."

His time for what?

Thinking nothing of it, he nodded at Bandile and set off on a hurried walk down the terminal.

It was his turn to save Eddie this time, though he had no clue how.

And as Bandile watched him leave, he realised what this whole experience had been for. It was the message he had been awaiting for so long.

Eddie had begun the calling of The Devil's Three.

"I'm sorry, Derek," he whispered. "I'm so, so sorry."

14

Eddie loved catching up with Jenny. With the way adult life was, they could go weeks, sometimes months, without being able to meet up – but when they did, it was like they have never even been apart.

"Lacy is doing great," Jenny was telling him. "She's been saving lives as a nurse, doing all that kind of stuff. Sometimes she comes home talking about a man she resuscitated that day, and I'm excited about having a new stapler in my office."

Eddie laughed and took a sip of his coffee.

"Then there's you," she continued, "who saves people from demons."

"And you, without whom, I would not have been able to save Derek," he reminded her. She blushed and smiled at him gratefully. "Don't put yourself down."

He looked around her kitchen and peered through the doorway to the living room. It was here that he had faced his first challenge, whilst living as a bum on their sofa bed.

Things have changed so much, he thought to himself.

Then he looked to his best friend sitting opposite and thought: *Actually, nothing has changed at all.*

"I'd better go." Eddie finished his last sip of coffee

and glanced at his watch. "Kelly is finding it really tough lately, and I don't want to leave her alone too long."

"She still that bad?"

"Think about what happened to her. She just keeps waking up screaming, remembering horrible things she had done."

"Oh man, that sucks. Look, if there's anything I can do…" she trailed off, taking Eddie's warm smile as acknowledgement. "We should double date again soon."

"I'd love that."

Jenny saw him to the door and they hugged, with promises of catching up again soon. He left, content with thoughts of friendship in his mind.

Walking home, he thought about how he could help Kelly, but concluded he was stuck. He'd experienced having an entity dwelling within his body very briefly when battling Balam, and for even longer as Lamashtu took him over; but had never dealt with the prolonged years of possession she'd had, passed off as a mental condition. Nor had he ever been occupied by something with such overwhelming power as she had.

He had fought his opponent and won. She was still fighting her battles.

Do I need to pass by the office for anything? Do we need any milk for the supermarket? Should I get a TV paper?

He felt a strong stab of guilt in the base of his belly. He was trying to find things to prevent him having to go home, because he didn't know how to face the issues Kelly was having. Normally, he was the one people brought to their houses for solutions to their demonic problems.

Not this time.

As he opened the door to his car he'd had to park around the corner from Jenny's house, he felt a soft brush against his right shin. Looking down, he saw a ginger tabby cat rubbing its body affectionately against his leg.

It must belong to someone in one of the local houses. Why on earth was it fussing him? He didn't know it.

Kneeling, he stretched out his hand and gave the cat a long brush down its back. It looked up to him and blinked its eyes, Eddie being sure that if it could smile that is what it would be doing.

It purred, and this made Eddie feel warm inside. A strange thing, how making an unknown feline purr can make feel a little triumphant. Smug, even, that an animal instinctively likes you.

It slumped itself on the floor, laying down and stretching out, Eddie tickling its belly.

Eddie moved his hand upwards to its head and gave it a fuss, tickling its neck. It stretched its head upwards, allowing its neck to come into full view so he could tickle it further.

He stretched his hand out and used the skin between his thumb and finger to stroke down its neck. Slowly, he stopped rubbing his hand downwards and placed his hand over its neck, hovering it there, lucidly looking at the cat below.

It stopped purring and looked up at him, unsure why he had stopped.

Eddie ignored its confusion, still hovering his hand over its throat. He applied a slight bit of pressure and the cat struggled, so he moved his knee onto its chest and knelt on it with the full force of his weight to hold the cat still.

He squeezed harder and harder, tightening the grip in his hand, feeling his fingers against its oesophagus, the solidity of its throat beneath its soft fur.

The cat struggled. Eddie didn't care. It couldn't squirm or squeal, Eddie was pressing too hard.

And it felt good.

Then, it went still.

Its body flopped.

The chest was no longer rising or deflating beneath his knee. The eyes of the cat were wide, like it knew.

Like it was aware that these were the last moments of its life.

For a while after the cat stopped struggling, Eddie remained firmly in his position, ensuring it was completely dead. Once he was sure, and not until that exact moment, he stood and opened his car door.

Switching the engine on with his right hand, he used his left hand to navigate the stereo to the radio. A happy song about sunshine was playing, so he turned it up loud and smiled, jigging along as pulled the car away and drove off.

15

Derek's legs bounced up and down uncontrollably, unable to shake his anxiety. He knew fretting would do nothing, nor would it speed the plane up, but he couldn't help it. He felt useless, floating 30,000 feet up in the air without anything to do.

What if Eddie had already killed? What if Derek was going to come back to find everyone he cared about destroyed? The neglected messiah present within Eddie latched onto his soul, taking control without Eddie having any idea.

Realising the woman next to him was staring at him out of annoyance that his leg was bouncing against hers, he tried to keep it still. He glanced up and down the aisle, not sure what he was looking for, but looking just the same.

"Excuse me," prompted the woman next to him, and he let her out, watching her walk down the plane to the toilet.

As an air hostess walked past with a trolley, he put his hand out.

"Excuse me, miss, could I have some water?" he requested, his throat dry and closed.

With a smile, she obliged. He opened it immediately and drank half the bottle in one. He checked his watch. It was hours until they were due in

London. It was a long flight from Cambodia.

As this thought entered his mind, he wondered, why had Bandile taken him to somewhere so far away from London? Surely he could have foreseen, or had some kind of feeling, that Derek would need to return?

Although Derek knew Bandile's visions didn't work like that, he couldn't help but feel hazy in his mind when it came to Bandile's foresight.

Bandile could have taken him to a more recent genocide where the devil still lingered. The Kurdish genocide in Iraq in 1986, maybe? The Bosnian genocide in 1992? The death toll was significantly lower, but they were still enormous atrocities nonetheless.

"Derek."

He shot his head around.

Someone was sitting next to him.

It was a familiar face. It took Derek a while to place it, but once he had, he could barely move.

"I thought you were dead?" Derek gasped.

"I am," replied the stone-cold face of Jason Aslan.

Derek's jaw hung open like a door without a lock. His mind thumped; he already had so many questions, then this rose so many more. How was he here?

"You are," Derek spoke in a paralysed whisper. "I saw your head severed from your body. I watched it happen."

"And I felt it happen, though I assure you, my head is very much on right now."

Derek held his hand out to touch him Jason. Could this be a trick of his mind? Anxiety's manifestation?

But Jason's shoulder felt firm under Derek's palm.

Derek's heart raced and his lungs expanded at a

million miles an hour.

It took only a second until Jason's shoulder burnt Derek's hand and he had to instantly withdraw it.

"What's going on?" Derek demanded. He willed himself to think clearly. He had faced difficult, inexplicable situations before.

"I am here from the master of hell," Jason spoke blankly.

"What?"

"Please, don't make this any more difficult…" Jason bowed his head and gathered himself.

"Make what any more difficult?"

"You can't let Eddie know that there's something inside of him. I'm sorry."

With a reluctant smile, Jason lifted his fist into the air.

"What are you going to do?"

Jason didn't answer. He simply pointed his raised fist down and, with that slightest of gestures, the plane tipped downwards, accelerating faster and faster.

They were going down. The plane was going down.

"*Stop it*!" Derek cried out. Around him were shrieks of fear, hostesses falling onto their backs and plummeting down the tilted floor of the capsized aeroplane.

"I can't."

Jason stood, looking down at Derek, who stared up at him helplessly. With a bow of Jason's head, he faded away.

The plane was plummeting harder and harder. The lights flickered. People screamed for their lives.

The oxygen masks plunged downwards and the

captain's voice came over the Tannoy.

"Ladies and gentlemen, we have lost control of the plane. Please assume crash positions."

Derek's eyes darted back and forth around the cabin.

People were in floods of tears.

Husbands. Wives. Mothers. Fathers. Friends.

Children.

All clinging onto each other, all clutching their loved ones.

Hysterical shrieks merged into the devastating scream of the plane's engine whirring out of control.

Everywhere Derek looked, people were preparing for death.

No, he decided.

He unfastened his seat belt and knelt on the back of the seat in front of him. The plane was almost at a full 180-degree tilt, plunging to its destruction.

The sound of the wings buckling consumed the room. A sudden jolt shoved the cabin on its side and the sight of a wing flying into distant fire hung in the periphery of the window.

Derek moved, dropping himself into the aisle and held onto a seat with both hands. He let go, tumbling with full ferocity, and slamming against the tilted door to the cockpit. His back ached from the slam, but he didn't have time to care.

Beside him was the hostess, in crash position, tears streaming down her eyes. Derek lifted his hand out and grabbed hers.

"Is there a parachute?"

She looked back at him, eyes blurred with water, unable to answer.

He crawled along the wall to the window beside

her. The clouds had disappeared and the sea was getting closer.

He threw his fist into the window with all the strength he could gather.

Nothing. It did nothing.

He tried it again. The window wouldn't break. Of course not. These things were designed to be tough.He rested. There was no way out. The plane was heading into the middle of the ocean and there was nothing he could do to escape.

With a desperate clamber, he reached for the seat next to the hostess and pulled himself to it. He tied the seat belt around his waist and held the oxygen mask in front of his mouth with his shaking hands.

I'm sorry Eddie.

"Everyone who does evil hates the light, and will not come into the light for fear that their deeds will be exposed."

John 3:20

16

1 January 2000

Millennium Night

"*Free my sister!*" Eddie screamed at the wicked beast before him.

"*I command you, bitch of hell. Release her!*"

Balam screeched, its voice caught on the wind of its spin. The room turned into a tornado of chaos, objects turning to weapons against Balam as they got caught in the circle of the whirlwind it created.

"It is done!" Balam replied, and Eddie dropped the girl's body to the floor.

From within it, a body rose. A translucent, vacantly existential, bare form of a spirit. But to Eddie, it was instantly recognisable.

Cassy was the spirit. Eddie's sister, stuck in child form for over a decade, forced to be tortured in hell for what seemed like an eternity.

He had freed her.

And her heart ached to see him on the floor, midst

of battle, in such pain.

She loved him so much. She was so grateful for what he had done. She had felt his pain, felt his love – even from within the evil heart of Balam's conjured form, she could see Eddie battling to free her.

The hurt that was done could never be undone. The suffering she had endured… endless nights that literally never ended; being suffocated by demons, stretched between them as they played, ripped open and fed upon her. Endless nights of rape, abuse, and torment. They had somehow kept her in a form of undead consciousness so she could still endure the excruciating agony the subjects of hell wished to inflict on her.

She had spent over a decade in hell. And now, thanks to her wonderful, wonderful brother, she was free. Free to leave the pain of hell and pass into heaven.

She hovered above Eddie for a moment. Eddie, her older brother, with whom she'd had an adolescence of growing up together robbed. Soon, she would be able to look back and relive his grief, his desperation to free her, his devastation at her parting.

"Eddie…" she whispered, holding her hand out toward him, a translucent entity he couldn't touch. "Thank you…"

He was gone.

As was her heavy body, the torn muscles, the aching lungs. All of it. Disappeared, along with the house.

When she next opened her eyes, she was in a field. Sun shone down at her with beautiful luminosity, green blades of grass leading to trees full of life, a gentle breeze soothing her delightfully empty body.

Is this heaven?

Taking her first steps through this new world, she smiled the first genuine smile she could remember. She felt older, wiser, like the mind-set she was meant to be. At peace, one with the environment painted around her.

She felt free.

"Cassy," came a safe, feminine voice behind her.

She spun around and feasted her eyes on a woman with long, straight, gorgeous brown hair and a smile that set her at ease.

"Cassy, you angel. You beauty. You saint," this woman asserted with a welcoming, elated grin. "You absolute saint. You truly are remarkable."

"What – what do you mean?" Cassy stammered. Her voice was no longer croaky, no longer weak.

"We have seen all you have endured, and we are sorry, but your brother… What he did for you. What you did for him. For love. It was… nothing short of remarkable. It was inhumanly powerful."

Cassy blushed.

"Is this… is this heaven?"

"This is heaven and you are very welcome here."

Finally.

"I…" Tears welled up in her eyes. "I'm so grateful…"

"No, we are grateful for *you*."

She wiped her eyes. This wasn't a time for crying. This was a time for rejoicing.

"Now, Cassy. We have a choice for you. Listen carefully."

Cassy nodded and focussed.

"If you wish, you can pass into heaven. You have

earnt it, after all. I will step aside, you will step forward, and you will stay there forever. Untouched."

"Okay…" Cassy wondered. A sinking feeling in her stomach left her unsettled about what the second option could be.

"The second option. Now, Cassy, you have earnt your place here, more so than most. But your brother is going to need your help. He is going to need you to intervene."

"Why?"

"On 25 July, 2002, at 3.00 a.m., there will be a ritual in attempt to raise hell. They will succeed."

"How can you know this?"

"We know. Trust us, Cassy. We've been doing this a long time."

She nodded.

"If you choose this option, you earn your place as an angel. As a saint. Someone of divine power. But you will be need to be involved. Without you… there is little hope."

"But – can't another angel do it?"

The woman shook her head. "I'm afraid not. It's hard to explain, Cassy."

Cassy closed her eyes and bowed her head. Just when she thought life was complete. When she was convinced her suffering would end.

"Like I said, you have a full pass to enter heaven, and you will not be held in contempt if you choose to turn the second option down. But I have a feeling, from what I have witnessed for the past years, you will struggle to."

"One question… if I don't do this… will my brother – will he die?"

"No."

Cassy breathed out a sigh of relief.

"It will be worse."

Her sigh abruptly ceased.

"He will become the antichrist. He will be the coming of the devil. He will end everything."

Cassy brushed her hands over her face, torn, her non-existent heart racing. She thought about heaven, thought about what could be, where she could end up, how she could be at peace.

But they both knew which choice she was going to make.

17

21 July 2002

One year seven months since the millennium

Martin sat at the table in silence, his mother staring absentmindedly at the floor, as usual.

He glared at her.

He loved her, yet he loathed her. And he felt guilty for it.

Of course, he wished he had a mother who would take care of him. Or maybe even a father who could take care of them both. But this was the hand he'd been dealt, and he would deal with it.

Having finished his beans on toast, he moved to the chair beside Anna and scooped her spoon through her beans.

"Y'need to eat, Ma," he told her, though she didn't react. He didn't expect her to. She was in one of her hazy, open-eyed sleeps.

He took a spoon full of beans and lifted it to her mouth, forcing it between her lips and dragging the spoon out against her teeth to ensure she ate it all.

The phone rang. Finding it a welcome relief, he stood up and answered it.

"Yeah?"

"Martin, it's Kristy."

His heart raced.

"Sup, Kristy."

"We goin' down park tonight, you in?"

He looked to his mother. Sitting there, dormant, vacant, catatonic.

"Sure, babe, what time?"

"Like, now."

"Now? I got to take care of me ma."

"Oh, come on," she moaned sexily. "I'm feeling well up for it…"

His eyes widened at her forthrightness.

"A'right, I'm comin'."

He hung up the phone and walked into the hallway, shoving his coat on. He felt bad for leaving his ma, but he couldn't just sit inside watching her do nothing all evening – not when there's a fitty on the line.

"I'm poppin' out, Ma," he called out as he returned to the kitchen.

He froze.

The light… It had been turned off.

How did she…?

She was still sat in her wheelchair, completely motionless. Except, her back was to him. Her wheelchair, and her, had turned completely the other way around.

"Ma?" he asked, cautiously.

He glanced at the light switch beside his head. She

was sat vacantly on the other side of the room. How had she managed to switch the light off without him noticing?

What's more, how the hell had she turned around? She could barely lift her legs. She couldn't even toilet herself, so how had she managed that?

"Ma?"

Martin took a step toward her and stopped.

"Ma? How'd you do that?"

A growl hissed throughout the room, silently teasing him with its faint sound.

Martin froze. His eyes scurried back and forth.

Something felt wrong.

"Ma? That you?"

Her hair blew with a draught of wind.

Martin was confused. The doors were closed, the windows were shut. There was no wind.

"Ma, what's going on?"

He took another marginal step forward. He was freaking.

How was she doing this?

That's when he saw it.

A faint silhouette, barely visible. Beside her. The black outline of claw, lifting in the shadows of the room.

It was dark and he couldn't be sure it wasn't a trick of the light, the trees brushing in the wind out the window and causing movement within the light. He was sceptically assured.

But he had seen *something*.

"Who's there?"

Another step.

He stood an arm's reach from her now. Still.

Examining every corner of the room.

A trickery of the mind, he decided. Tiredness mixed with an illusion of light bouncing against the wall.

"It's not real," he told himself.

As if reacting to his disbelief, the shadow grew large in a visible growl of anger. It encompassed the room, taking over his mum, spreading toward him at an aggressive speed.

He darted backwards and whacked his hand against the light, filling the room with the power of a single light bulb.

There was nothing.

No creature. No beast, no sound. No nothing.

Just him and Ma.

He edged forward and knelt in front of her. Her head had dropped against her shoulder, her eyes shut tight. She was snoring.

He ran his hand down her hair and stood back up, looking around. He wasn't sure what he had witnessed, but he knew there must be some other explanation.

Without any reluctance, he bolted to the door, stuffed the house keys in his pocket and left.

He really needed to go out and get fucked with Kristy, for his own good.

18

Kelly sat motionless beside an untouched mug of tea. She didn't even move as she heard the front door open and close.

The entrails of the cat dangling from its decapitated head played in her mind like a movie on a loop. She could still smell the decaying meat mixed with the stench of death. Her eyes barely blinked. Her breathing was exhaustive, quick but wheezing; each intake of oxygen getting caught in her throat.

Eddie dropped his bag, ran up to her and put his arms around her.

"Kelly, are you okay?" he gasped.

She forced her eyes closed. She couldn't look at him, couldn't bear it.

What was he going to say when he saw it? How would he react?

"Kelly?" he prompted once more.

She knew she had to respond, but she could not force her mouth open. The muscles in her mouth couldn't move. Wedging her eyes tightly shut, she winced as the image played in her mind once more.

"Kelly, please, talk to me. Was it another dream?"

It took all she had to force her head to shake the slightest bit.

She willed herself to speak, filled her head with

tension until her mouth finally opened and she could murmur a few words.

"Look… The shed…" she mustered.

She didn't open her eyes, but she could feel him rush to the garden. As the back door opened, she felt the cold draught carrying the foul odour back into the room and flying it to every corner.

Her eyes squeezed shut with all her might. Her heart raced, her fists clenched and her leg bounced with severe agitation.

The shed door creaked open.

The scream of shock from Eddie's voice.

The silence of his terror reverberating through the peaceful night sky.

As he walked back into the room and sat in silence beside her, she found a tinge of comfort in his horror. Enough, at least, that she could open her eyes and look at him.

"The Latin…" he uttered, staring at anything but Kelly. "It means –"

"Rise, devil," Kelly interrupted.

He gradually rotated his head toward her and they held eye contact, sharing a moment of stunned confoundment.

"Did you…?" he asked. Even though Kelly had expected the question, it still hurt a little bit.

"No," she shook her head, speaking softly. "Not that I'm aware of."

An uncomfortable moment of stillness hovered between them.

"Did you?" Kelly asked, bringing herself to ask the question.

"God, no," Eddie frowned. "Why would you…?"

"I don't know." Kelly bowed her head. "A hunch."

"A hunch?"

"You faced the devil. That's got to do something to you."

"Yeah, and you had the devil in you, so –"

Eddie abruptly left the table. An argument was not what they needed.

Running his hands over his face and through his hair, he found himself approaching the sink. He took a glass, filled it with water, and drank it so fast it spilled down his chin.

"Are we safe?" Kelly leant forward, scared about the question she didn't want to ask and the answer she didn't want to hear. "I mean, if someone's doing this… are we safe? Here?"

"If someone is targeting us, Kelly, then where we are is irrelevant."

"But someone *is* targeting us," Kelly adamantly pointed out. "We know that. Someone from hell who wants you to be his messiah on earth."

Eddie remained still, leaning over the sink, staring down the plug hole into God knows where.

Kelly watched him, waiting, until she eventually gave up hoping for an answer.

"I'll clean it up," Eddie quietly decided. "I'll meet you in bed."

He grabbed a bin bag from under the sink and burst out of the room and into the garden, shutting the door behind him.

Kelly meandered upstairs, dizzy, steadying herself on the bannister. She made it to the bathroom and absentmindedly brushed her teeth. She must have been there for nearly ten minutes, just going back and forth over the same tooth.

When she entered the bedroom, she hovered by the

window to see if she could spot Eddie outside. The cat's head was wrapped in a plastic bag on the lawn and Eddie was scrubbing at the blood with plastic gloves on and a scourer in his hand.

She climbed into bed and lay on her side, staring at the wall in front of her. She was not the least bit tired.

And even if she was tired, there was no way she wanted to close her eyes and dream about this.

19

21 July 2002

The ceiling above Eddie was a tediously familiar sight. He lay awake, staring at the faded white above him.

Kelly finally slept, though she was far from peaceful. She was murmuring, tossing and turning, muttering cries. He considered waking her, but decided that she needed to sleep, even if it was a restless sleep. She would be haunted by her mind if she was awake, too; may as well let her be haunted by it while she rests.

He turned his head to the alarm clock and blinked his eyes into focus. 00.30 a.m. They had only been in bed for two hours.

It felt like he had been laid there for days.

A cat's head, nailed to the wall of the shed, with the words 'Rise devil' written in Latin. Evidently whoever did it couldn't have had access to their house, or they would have done it inside. Or maybe whoever did it wanted to startle them, whilst allowing a fragile sense of security.

He decided this was nonsense. There was no sense

of security left. The head of an animal outside your home was a very clear message.

Either way, he decided he wasn't going to sleep, nor did he really want to, so he gave up. He'd go downstairs, have a glass of milk, maybe even get some work done. Whatever it took to keep his mind occupied; he couldn't lay in bed staring wide-eyed at the ceiling any longer.

As he leant up and reached for his t-shirt, Kelly turned and brushed against him with her arm.

"No, leave, help, I don't…" she mumbled, her sleep-talking fading into indecipherable mutters.

He stood next to the bed, watching her, wondering what could be going on in her mind. Was it another flashback? Another recollection that would continue to haunt her conscious mind when she finally awoke from her unoccupied torment?

"Three… Three…" she repeated. "Three…"

Three?

"The Devil's Three…" The muttering stopped and her speech became clearly audible.

"The what?" Eddie asked, not knowing what answer he was going to get.

"The Devil's Three…" she repeated, rocking back and forth.

"The De –"

"The Devil's Three!" she sat bolt upright and screamed at the top of her lungs. Eddie flung himself against the far wall and gawked at her.

Her body relaxed and she lay back down, her closed eyes not even flickering. Her talking subsided and she finally rested peacefully.

Eddie didn't move. He stood still, his arms stiffened, his legs frozen, his eyes fixated on her.

The Devil's Three?

It was what she had said. Definitely. It must be something of significance, something left over from the days of her possession, something buried in the back of her mind.

But what could it be?

Eddie couldn't recollect any reference to The Devil's Three. He had much experience with the blabbering of demons and the stuff they come out with through the helpless mouths of their victims. Such a title seemed important, something that would have made an impression, but he had no prominent memory presenting itself.

He slowly creaked the bedroom door open, careful not to wake Kelly. Treading lightly on the floorboards, he made his way to the stairs, lightly tapping down each step and toward his book-case.

Most of his books were at the university, but he kept the most important ones at home. What's more, he kept the most dangerous ones at home; anything that had reference to the devil could not be left anywhere one of his students could access it. It was too much of a risk that someone may take it, even by mistake. Who knows what they might do with it in some drunken escapade when they've had too many beers on a Friday night and they see the book lying around their kitchen.

His finger hovered past the top row of books. They were organised so the heavier subjects were toward the bottom, but he wanted to be thorough, make sure he withdrew any book that may help him.

Once he reached the books on the occult on the penultimate row, he withdrew a few that he knew had references to the devil. They were old, tattered books, written in times long ago when everyone believed in superstitions. It was often hard to separate the books that were genuine from the majority that were ramblings of knowledge from a time when people knew no better. Most of the relevant books, however, would be on this book case.

History of the Occult was the first he took out. On top of that he placed *Satanists Through History* and *Occult Leaders Who Devil Worship*.

He withdrew most of the books from the bottom row – as this was the collection that focussed on the devil and Satanism. He tossed a few to the side and flicked through the ones he thought might be most relevant.

Nothing in the chapters, or indexes, or pages he skimmed, showed anything. Not even *The Devil Lives: Satanism Rituals Used Throughout History* had any reference to The Devil's Three. Nor did the next book, or the next, or the next.

Before he knew it, an hour had gone by and the final book he had withdrawn lay open before him.

Nothing.

Maybe he just needed a more thorough search?

No. He generally knew what was in these books. If there was something relevant, he would have found it.

But there wasn't.

And he'd had a feeling from the beginning he would not find what he was looking for.

Closing his eyes, he racked his brain.

Think. The Devil's Three… Surely it's referred to somewhere…

Then it hit him – Derek's study. Derek had a huge collection of books on the paranormal in his house, and it would undoubtedly be the best place to search.

Putting on a pair of jeans over his pyjama shorts and a coat he found draped over the sofa, he grabbed a notepad and wrote a note for Kelly.

Kel – gone to Derek's to use his books, I think I'm on to something.

Hoped you slept well. Love you.

Eddie.

He re-read it, then added four kisses – he needed to make sure she knew he was there for her, that he cared, no matter what.

Grabbing Derek's spare house keys, Eddie bolted out of the front door. As he thought about Derek's impressive collection of books, he wondered where Derek was, and whether Derek was having any success in finding answers.

Eddie hoped he would hear from him soon.

20

The full moon shone bright in the sky, like a distant disturbance forewarning Martin of something he couldn't figure out. He only caught a glimpse of the moon through the bed sheets, but it stuck in his mind, distracting him.

Simon's empty house. Simon's parents' bedroom. It felt a bit wrong. Simon shared a room with his brother, and he was using that one with whatshername, so Martin didn't have much choice.

But it was still a distraction.

Shut up he told himself.

Kristy was on top of him. Topless. Grinding. Dry humping his painfully stiff cock.

She was so fit. The kind of fit that made your head spin round and explode.

And here he was. Underneath her. About to possibly, maybe, could – fuck her.

But the moon through the window. That's what he was thinking about.

Dick head. Forget about the shitty moon, you twat.

She threw her head downwards, pushing her lips against his so aggressively it hurt. He didn't care. He loved it. Her hair was falling over him and draping around them, cocooning their heads into their own small space.

He stroked his hands down her back, brushing her bra strap.

Shit! Should I take it off?

Thing is, he'd never taken one off before. He was kind of waiting for her, but had the feeling she was kind of waiting for him.

Fuck it. Gonna go for it.

After he fiddled for a few uncomfortable seconds, she giggled, lifted herself up and undid her own bra, freeing her breasts, and flinging their prison onto the floor beside his t-shirt.

She smirked at his gawking eyes. He felt momentarily humiliated at the chuckles about his fumbling bra method – but the sight of her topless was enough to force those thoughts from his mind.

This is what he wanted. What he had wanted for ages.

She giggled playfully as she unbuttoned her skirt, unzipped it right down to the bottom – not that there was much of it – and threw it to the floor.

Now she was grinding him. Grinding in nothing but a lacy, red thong.

This was a dream. Better than his imagination could conjure. Better than any of the stupid pornos he'd watched.

She was gorgeous, naked, and riding him like there was no tomorrow.

That's when his mother's face came into his head.

She would be stuck downstairs. Sleeping in her chair because he hadn't helped her up. Pissing herself.

Why am I thinking of my fucking mum pissing herself? Get a grip!

He felt guilty, but he was fifteen; he deserved a night off, a night he got to fool around with a girl, like every other teenager does.

A night where he got to fuck the hot, blond, naked girl leaving a wet patch over his zipper – without feeling bad about it.

"Aren't you gonna take off your trousers?"

She bowed her head lustily, her curly locks falling in front of her face and landing over her perfect C-cup breasts.

"Er…" he stuttered.

Without a second thought, he hastily undid his belt and slid his trousers down. She passionately grasped the sides of his trouser legs, dragging them to his feet, pulling them off and throwing them to the floor.

She rose back up with a naughty smile and a kinky twinkle in her eye. Her lips pursed with frisky arousal as she looked down upon his rigid erection. Before Martin could do anything else, she had placed the whole thing in her mouth.

He grabbed the pillow behind his head and yelped. It felt warm. Wet. Heavenly.

She moved her head up and down, rubbing her tongue along his dick as her lips brushed firmly against him.

What if I come?

He grabbed hold of her hair, halting her for a second. She looked up and grinned, taking it as her cue to climb on top of him.

"I – I don't know what to do."

What the fuck?

Why am I saying that? Why am I telling this girl I didn't know what to do? What is wrong with me?

She just smiled, grabbed a hold of him and placed him inside of her, closing her eyes and fluttering them as she did.

It felt warm. Warm and moist.

She moved up and down and it felt so good and his immediate thought was – *oh my God. Is this it? Am I no longer a virgin?*

And just as it started to feel even better, his mum sprang back into his mind.

He could see her, alone in the kitchen, saliva dribbling down her lip. Alone. Stinking of piss.

He shouldn't have left her. And he knew it. And this was guilt, in the best moment of his life so far – a blissfully divine moment ruined by guilt.

Before he could think any more or enjoy the grinding any more, the door burst open and Simon jumped in, the girl he had been shagging trailing behind him. A huge, freezing streak of water fired at Martin's face and he turned away, feeling Kristy move herself off him and fall to the floor.

He collapsed beside her, clutching his hand over his head, protecting himself from the icy blasts that kept going.

Once the spray of water had stopped, Martin peered over the bed. Simon was standing there, a grin spread across his face, laughing hysterically, like a hyena in its element. He held a Super-Soaker water gun pointed in Martin's direction.

"What the fuck man!" Martin screamed out, but it was drowned out by the sound of laughter.

Next to him was Kristy, soaked, naked. Her body, which was supposed to only be meant for him, was now seen by his best mate and that girl and he couldn't take it. They shouldn't be seeing it.

But she was laughing too.

Kristy was guffawing uncontrollably. Everyone was. Everyone but Martin.

This was the best moment of his life, the moment he had been waiting for forever, the moment he had blown off his sick mum for and – they were laughing.

Even Kristy. And that hurt.

She didn't care if it hurt.

She just laughed.

She looked directly into his eyes and laughed.

"What the fuck is your problem, you dick head?" he screamed at Simon as he got to his feet and pulled his underwear and trousers back on.

"You!" Simon sputtered out breathlessly between helpless hysterics, barely able to keep his balance amongst all the laughter. "You should have seen your face!"

Another look at Kristy. Laughing. Rolling around on the floor. Naked. Her body that was only meant for him jiggling about in front of everyone.

Simon. Pointing at her and laughing. Pointing at him and laughing. The girl he'd shagged behind him laughing like the little slut he decided she was.

"You're such a prick!" Martin reinforced.

"You should have seen your face, mate!" Simon continued. "You looked like your mum after she shat herself!"

That was it.

He couldn't help it. He saw red. Everything drowned out into blackness and before he knew it he had pulled his fist back and landed it into Simon's face. He didn't even realise what he was doing until he was on top of him, punching repeatedly, landing his fist into Simon's bloody face again and again and again.

Kristy pulled at his arm, her begging for him to stop a distant voice in the darkness. That skank who

Simon had shagged backed up against the wall, not getting involved, not invested in Simon enough to stand up for him.

The laughter had stopped. At least that fucking laughter had stopped.

"Stop!" he finally heard Kristy shout into his ear, and he stood up.

Panting. Looking down at Simon. A bloody mess. Simon looking up at Martin.

Without a second thought, Simon burst to his feet and pushed Martin backwards. Martin stumbled and hit the wall and Simon threw a punch at him, which missed.

Martin backed up further.

"Get out of my fucking house!" demanded Simon.

Martin grabbed a hold of his t-shirt, jacket, and shoes and paced to the door.

He took one more moment to look back at Kristy. She was in the corner of the room, covering her body with her hands.

Now she covers her body!

She looked scared. Intimidated. Weak.

She looked like his mum used to when his dad got cross when he was a kid.

He kicked the door open and marched downstairs. Pausing by the door to put his shoes on, he left the house, slamming the door behind him. He marched down the street lit by street-lights, putting on his t-shirt and jacket.

There went his best friend. His potential girlfriend.

There went the only things he had in his life beside his mum.

What was the point?

Why bother with any of this?

He walked home with his hands in his pockets and put his mum to bed. Afterwards, he laid in his bed all night, staring at the ceiling, trying to think of one thing he had to live for beside his mum.

21

Eddie huddled his coat around himself. Despite being summer, the nights were still windy and mild. What's more, the whole Devil's Three thing was giving him a bit of a chill.

That is what she said, right? 'Devil's Three'? he questioned himself.

He replayed the scene in his head, Kelly beside him, angrily blabbering in her sleep, then – yes, she had shouted it, clear as day. It was the only thing she had said that he could clearly make out, and her words had been particularly precise.

He took Derek's spare key out of his pocket and placed it into the door, twisting the first lock, then the second, and gently pushing the door open. It creaked to a dark, cold, empty house.

Closing the door behind him, he switched on the light and removed his shoes. Funny, even though Derek was off on his search for wisdom in some far-off country, he still felt the pressing need to be polite and remove his shoes.

Derek's study was the coldest room in the house. Eddie turned on the light and the radiator, to find neither any heat or lights working. Derek must have switched the heating off, which made Eddie feel a little tinge of sadness – it meant Derek planned to be away for a while.

He missed him. He needed him. If only he'd get in contact somehow. He'd write to him, if only he knew where to send the letter.

Nevertheless, Eddie tucked his coat around himself and embraced the cold damp in the air. Glancing at his watch, he saw that it was gone 5.00 a.m. and he would likely need to 'get up' for work in a few hours.

He wondered if Kelly was even aware that he had left the bed beside her.

Scouring the bookshelf, he found Derek's restricted section at the top. Pulling the chair out from the desk behind him, he climbed upon it and looked across the books. All of them referenced dark paranormal activity and the occult. Once he had come to a book entitled *The Devil's Rituals Vol 2*, he took it out and climbed back down.

He took himself into the kitchen to make a cup of tea and carelessly threw the book onto the dining table. He felt a stab of guilt over how much Derek would hate him for daring to abuse one of his precious books.

Then he decided, *fuck him.*

He wasn't there.

He hadn't even bothered to let him know where he was, or the progress of his search.

He had no idea if he was even still alive. It was a thought that chilled him, until he decided that a man who had taken on the depths of hell for a living was unlikely to be beaten by anything on this earth.

After the kettle clicked, he poured the hot water over a tea bag and let it settle. He gazed at the water as it gradually turned brown. His head dripped off into a distant haze as his tiredness hit him.

He snapped himself back out of it, removed the tea bag and went to add milk, before realising there would be none. Black tea it was.

Settling himself down in front of the book, he set the cup of tea beside him to let it cool. He skimmed the contents, finding nothing about the Devil's Three. Slumping the pages of the thick book to the other side, he skimmed the index.

That's where he found it.

Devil's Three, rituals, page eighty-nine.

He flicked the pages through, slowing down as he got to page seventy, allowing the next few pages to trickle through his hand. He landed on a brown, aged drawing accompanied by italic writing beneath it.

The drawing featured three figures gathered around a pile of dead animals. It was an old illustration; Eddie wasn't sure how old, but it reminded him of Bible illustrations he had read, used hundreds of years ago, made to teach young people about the Genesis story.

With a wide-eyed, unfaltering gaze, his eyes became glued to the words as he read them.

The Devil's Three

Also known as 'the threesome of sin.'

A ritual designed in purpose to bring forth the devil into the flesh of his intended. The ceremony is known to be commonly unsuccessful, but not because it doesn't work. It is said that the devil hears every attempt at this ritual, but chooses those sinners blessed enough for his presence.

The ritual requires the three to collect dead animals and a person who is said to be close to the devil as an offering.

The ritual is performed in a location of significance to the devil, such as the house of one of his victims, or one who has sinned greatly enough to attract his attention.

The ritual must then be performed by three people. Each person selected will fulfil one of these requirements:

The wounded.

The dead.

The prophet.

It is up to the sinners as to how they interpret the devil's three – but it is essential to get it right to show that you are worthy.

Eddie leant back. His hands drummed on the side of his cup. He remained still, contemplative, allowing the words to sink in.

It was a lot of information. Things became slightly clearer, but as they did, he became unsettled.

A ritual to bring forth the devil?

He and Kelly were in danger.

If someone was carrying out this ritual – Eddie still didn't know for definite if anyone was, but presumed that if Kelly was dreaming it, someone must be – then they needed the location of someone linked to the devil. As well as a sacrifice. And dead animals.

Dead animals, like the one in his shed.

And a sacrifice. They need to sacrifice someone who had been close to the devil…

He had a strong link to the devil – he was meant to be the instigator of hell on earth.

But surely it can't be me? They couldn't kill me, as they want me to become the heir to hell…

What about Kelly?

Kelly had been the only human alive Eddie knew to have been possessed by the devil.

What about The Devil's Three themselves?

Three people were needed to perform the ceremony: the wounded, the dead, and the prophet.

Who were they? And how does someone who's dead perform a ceremony?

There were so many questions filling his mind, he felt like they were all going to pour out until he lost track of them. There was too much he didn't know.

Then there was the most pertinent question of all: why was Kelly speaking this in her sleep?

If he was at all tired, that had gone, and he was filled with unpalpable terror. He hadn't a clue what to do or where to go.

He needed Derek.

Tucking the book under his arm, he poured the cup of tea into the sink and left.

What if the ceremony did happen? And it was successful? Then Derek returned after this happened?

If the ritual could bring forth the devil, surely it could also bring forth part of the devil? Or a piece of evil, planted by the devil? Or, if the devil was risen, it could surely bring around the part of evil within me far easier?

Eddie realised in that moment that, despite having the answer written in the book he clutched in his hands – he was still no closer to understanding what it all meant.

22

Eddie drove as fast as he could. His mind was full of questions and was aching profusely, but he couldn't rest.

Not now. Not with what he knew.

Soaring down a country lane, his lights on full beam, he knew he was driving dangerously.

But he didn't care.

He truly did not care.

What if someone got hurt? So what?

Fuck it.

He thought about Kelly, and what this meant for her. He thought about those nights in the hospital when she was admitted following her possession. Those nights he would wake up to find himself still in the chair beside her bed, her hand in his.

Those thoughts disappeared.

They were replaced with thoughts of his childhood.

His arsehole father.

His neglectful mother.

His dead sister.

Cassy. Oh God, Cassy. How he missed her. How much he wished she was still there. Not a day went by that she didn't cross his thoughts.

It was his stupid fucking fault she was dead. He

was the prick, the arsehole, the bastard. He was racing his bike. She was trying to impress him.

It was his fault.

My fault.

It was his arsehole dad's fault he turned out such a let-down. Sure, he was this great exorcist now. But he had been an alcoholic bum sleeping on his best friend's sofa for so long.

It was his dad's fault.

No, it was his mother's fault.

She was the one who sat there crying whilst his dad beat the shit out of Eddie. She was the one who never cared enough to stop it from happening.

Why? Because she was some dipshit coward?

Yes. And because she knew she was next.

Just delaying the inevitable, weren't you?

Those black eyes she covered up for him, those days she kept him back from school so the teachers didn't see the bruises. She covered it up. She let Eddie's dad get away with it.

And he hated him.

He hated her.

He fucking hated everything.

He was filled with rage, ready to punch something. Kill something. Burn something.

He was nearing eighty miles per hour. He needed to stop.

Pulling over to the side of the road and putting his hazards on, he buried his head into his shaking hands. His legs were quivering, his heart beating with fury. Everything and anything was shit.

His fist landed into the steering wheel and he kicked the car door open.

There was a man at the bus stop. A homeless man. Under a blanket. Some lazy piece of crap leeching off society. Some idiot prick who didn't care enough to get his own job.

Eddie marched across the road and put his hands around this guy's neck. The bum woke up quickly, but was too lethargic to react.

Probably on drugs, the selfish little arsehole.

Eddie threw the bum to the floor and kicked the guy in the face.

He kicked. And kicked. And kicked. And kicked.

Then he froze.

What was he doing?

Why was he so angry?

Why the hell am I beating the hell out of some random homeless guy?

Eddie backed up against the wall of the bus shelter. The homeless man was cowering on the floor, his arms covering his head in terror, sobbing helplessly.

What the hell is going on? Eddie demanded of himself.

His panting subsided. His heart slowed. His thoughts became clearer.

He had just gotten himself worked up, full of fury, over what? Memories? Feelings resurfacing?

He had been so angry.

They weren't his feelings.

But they were, at the same time.

This didn't make sense.

None of it made sense.

He knelt down beside the homeless guy, and placed a soft hand on the man's back. The homeless guy flinched and cowered away.

"I'm sorry..." Eddie asserted, his face full of sorrow, no idea how or why he had come to do such a thing.

"Please..." cowered the man. "Please just leave me alone..."

"My God," Eddie gasped to himself again. "I am so sorry."

He stood up, his hands cupped around his mouth in shock at what he had done. He'd never done anything like this before. He'd barely even been in a fight, except with a demon. He'd maybe gotten beaten up as a kid, but had never been in a two-way contest.

And now this.

He sprinted to his car, turned the hazards off and drove away, making sure to stay under the speed limit.

The whole way home, the thought continuously racked his mind.

What the hell did I just do?

23

Martin trudged through the peeling, creativity-killing, blank walls of the school, his hands in his hoodie pockets and his hood over his head. He didn't want anyone to see him, and he did not want to see anyone. Least of all anyone in this wretched school that he couldn't wait to leave in a matter of months.

Everyone was just constantly banging on about how the GCSEs were looming, coming closer, their future awaiting.

Martin couldn't give a shit.

The only reason he was there was because they threatened to fine his mum if he didn't stop truanting – and that was the last thing they needed.

Blanking some old, bald, up-his-arse teacher who barked at him to remove his hoodie ("that is not part of the school uniform, lad!" *Who gives a crap?*) he turned his direction away from the building and toward the cages where all the lads played football.

Thwack!

Martin was sent flying to the ground, as if a room full of weights had capsized into his back.

As he regained his awareness, he looked around to see a ball bouncing away from him, and a familiar pair of scruffy shoes marching toward him. They were the same pair Simon had worn for the past four years, because his mum was a cheap bitch not interested in spending any money on anything that didn't get her drunk or high.

Looking up, he saw Simon wasn't alone. There were a group of lads with him, lads Martin had spent time with at house parties but never really become acquainted with.

Kristy was there too. Somewhere in the crowd, a big grin on her face, enjoying every moment.

Martin stood up. Simon shoved him, in an attempt to force him back to the floor, but Martin shoved the hand away. Martin squared up to Simon, within an inch of his face, pushing him back.

"What?" Martin grunted.

His leg went out from behind him with an enormous surge of pain and he went flailing to his knees. Glancing over his shoulder, he saw some scumbag with his hair greased to his forehead withdrawing the foot he'd used to kick him with, laughing with his mates.

"Look at this lads, 'e's on 'is knees!" Simon cackled, leering down at Martin.

Martin's anger consumed him, heaving to his fists, spurring him into a frenzy. He attempted to unleash his rage on his former best friend. He leapt up and sent a punch sailing toward Simon's face, but was halted by a flying kick straight into his ribs from some other guy on his left.

As Martin bent over, disorientated from the pain, Simon's started bombarding him with thumps. Fist after fist laid into Martin's face, sending Martin onto his back, where he stayed.

Martin curled himself up into a ball, covering his head with his hand, as a group of dickheads laid their feet into any part of him they could harm.

His ribs, his neck, his shin, his face.

Anything.

They were all laughing. Every one of them. It was a chorus of humility, getting louder and louder.

But the things that hurt him far more than any kicks, the one hysterical laugh that stuck out from it all, the one that really pierced his heart – was the one coming from a female voice.

The laugh he recognised as Kristy's.

The kicking abruptly ceased and his attackers dispersed. Echoes of "teacher's coming" mirrored the urgency of their hasty departure.

No teacher came. No loyal student stayed. No one came rushing to his side.

Just as he expected.

He was all alone, laying on the floor, clutching onto his ribs with one hand and his face with the other.

He dabbed his face, glancing at the blood from his lip in his hand. He clambered to his feet, finding himself only able to put his weight onto one of his legs; his other shin was too wounded to move, and his knee was in seizing agony whenever he attempted to lift it.

Groggily moving forward and scrunching up his face in anguish, he limped his way into the building and through the doors to the boy's toilets.

The reflection in the mirror made him flinch. It was a bloody, humiliated mess. Barely recognisable as his own.

He thought about Kristy seeing this face. He saw her laughing at it, in stitches over his pained misery.

Switching the tap on and cupping his hands, he

lifted the water over his face. Beneath the blood was only mild bruising, meaning it wasn't obvious what had happened; which was good, as it would save him some pride.

It would save him having to explain to everyone that he just got the shit kicked out of him by his best mate while his girlfriend cackled in joy.

Lifting his top to expose his wounded chest, he flinched at the sight of a large, grey bruise across his right ribs. It explained the agony he was enduring in his torso, but at least that could be covered.

At least he didn't have to explain anything to his mum.

Then he remembered the warning letter to his mum. The part that said if he wasn't punctual to lessons, they could still get fined. The bell had gone ages ago.

"Shit."

But surely they would understand?

Understand what? He was hardly going to tell them, was he?

He brushed the door open and limped through the corridor. He planned to just sit there through double maths without attracting attention. Just keep his head down and shut up.

Making his way up a few steps was difficult; but hurriedly making his way up three flights of stairs was impossible. The strenuous pain was constant. He told himself to be a man, put up with it. Deal. So he had a few beatings; don't most men at some point in their life?

This was just a lesson about who to trust.

As he opened the door to the maths room, following a long, tedious ascent up the wooden stairs that practically fell apart beneath him, the entire class turned and looked at him.

Including Kristy, whose grin couldn't have been any bigger.

"Martin," observed the teacher in an irritably haughty voice. He couldn't even remember the guy's name; his hair was grey, he wore an embarrassing green tank top over a small pot belly and pulled an expression like someone had just shit in his breakfast. "Why are you late?"

Martin glanced once more at Kristy.

"Couldn't find the room," he made up, looking to his feet.

"Well, as fleeting as your appearances here have been, you have still been coming here for five years, and I undoubtedly believe that you are able to find the maths room on time."

Martin looked blankly back at him. He had nothing to say. He barely understood a word of what the teacher had said, to be honest.

"Remove your hoodie before you enter," the teacher commanded and turned back to the class.

If he removed the hoodie they would see the bruising on his face.

Kristy would see the bruising on his face.

He couldn't do it.

He just wanted to get to the back of the classroom and keep his head down silently. Why couldn't this teacher just let him do that?

"I ain't removing my hoodie."

"Yes you are."

"No, I ain't."

The teacher's eyes widened and his hair practically stood on end. Had this guy ever heard of a comb? He placed his text-book on the table and turned fully toward Martin, as if bracing for unleashing hell.

"You are in this school, are you not? In body if not mind?"

"I guess."

"Then you will follow its rules. We do not allow hoodies as part of our uniform. You are lucky I am not confiscating it. Now take it off before you enter my classroom."

"Why?"

"Why what?"

"Why do I need to take it off? It's hardly going to affect my learning, or your shitty lesson."

As soon as he said the word "shitty," he knew he'd done it. No turning back. His place there was under threat.

Good. They can exclude me then. Give me some days off without fining my disabled mum, you bunch of pricks.

"Martin, I don't know who you think you are, other than an insolent little child –"

"Don't call me that!"

"What? Insolent? Child? Which one of these things do you disagree with, Martin?"

"Why you gotta be such a dick, man? What are you getting out of this?"

"Grey hair, most likely," the teacher quipped, smirking in a hugely infuriating way.

"Oh, you're fuckin' funny, ain't yuh?" Martin raised his voice, his head nodding with annoyance, his arms shaking, his legs exchanging balance from one to the other, the pain in his body replaced with adrenaline.

"Excuse me?"

"My life ain't no fuckin' joke, dick head," Martin continued. "As for your education, you can stuff it up your bellend."

"Do you know who –"

"Who what? I woke up this mornin', then fed, toileted, washed my mum, then happened to put a hoodie on after I'd spent two hours doing that. Then I come here and you all tell me what to fuckin' do, like you have any idea what life is like."

"Look –"

"Nah, you look. You can stuff your shitty education, mate. I ain't in need of none of it."

Martin turned his back on the classroom and marched down the stairs. He could feel his furious flinching sneer stuck to his face. His lip stung, his ribs throbbed and his knee agonised.

But he didn't care.

He just didn't care anymore.

These people had no idea what it was like for him. So he was supposed to leave his mum to take of herself when she can't even feed or go to the toilet, so he can go to this building and get a poor excuse for an education?

Those people could afford a carer; not that they'd ever care enough to help get one for him.

They couldn't understand.

He was the carer. And that was all he had.

He burst the doors to the school open and stormed out, not even thinking about looking back.

24

A beetle scurried over Jason's chest. Despite being dead, his physique had not improved in an angelic or demonic way. His bare torso still hung off him with the fading of age. The ground beneath him bumped into his back, the heat of the minute stones burning his skin.

He weakly raised his head, kneeling on his arms, looking down upon himself. He had no idea how he got wherever he was, nor did he understand why he wore nothing but ragged shorts, ripped and shredded over his skin.

"Granddaddy?" came the familiar voice of Ava behind him. Wrath crawled under his skin, bumping up to his mind and filling him with rage.

He threw himself to his feet and turned to see the body and face of his granddaughter gazing up at him. His stomach twisted into knots; seeing a person he loved so much was even worse than his eternity in painful solace.

It was evil. Evil taking on the form of beauty. It was sinisterly poetic, almost; the angelic form consumed with self-indulgent malevolence.

"She never called me Granddaddy," Jason spat. "It was Grandad or Papa."

"Sorry, Papa," it smiled sweetly.

"You are not her. So you call me neither."

He stretched his aching muscles, turning his head, surveying the everlasting malicious horizon beyond him. They were on a stone mound, surrounded by a landscape of spewing lava.

"Where is this?"

"Hell." So direct, so matter of fact, so dismissive. Nothing like Ava at all.

"What do you want with me?" Jason whimpered through his detestation, forcing his anger to take the forefront, masking his despair. "I did what you asked."

"You did *some* of what he asked. You still have one more thing."

He flung his head backwards, grappling his hands over his head and through his hair.

More?

"*What more do you want from me?*" he screamed, flinging his arms outwards to emphasise his fury. His words reverberated back to him again and again and again. "I did every damn thing you wanted. I crashed that plane. I did it. What else?"

"Your final task."

"Why…" he cried, the pain consuming him. "Why can't you take someone else's form? Please stop using her face…"

"I will stop once you are done."

His emotions fluttered back and forth like a flickering light. One moment he was filled to the core with rage, then filled with love for the face of his granddaughter, then filled with desolation and anguish at the sheer loss of control.

"I can't… I can't take this…"

"You can and you will. You have one more task."

"No."

"You will do one more thing or I will stay like this and torment you forever. Then you and your family will suffer an eternity in hell. Is that what you want?"

Jason fell to his knees, covering his face in his hands. He cried. Cried like no one was watching. Like there was no other way he could manage his emotions.

He had spent his life proving against the paranormal, debunking the actual truth. He was spending his afterlife haunted by those he never believed in. A whole afterlife held captive by his invisible enemy.

When would he find some peace?

When would he be released?

When would they stop tormenting him with the face of someone he missed more than the oxygen that no longer filled his lungs?

"What?" He shook his head, sobbing through his tears, speaking delicately. "What do you wish me to do?"

"The Devil's Three."

"What?"

The beast wearing Ava's face took another step toward him.

"You must be one of The Devil's Three. You will take the place of the one who is dead. You will help him rise."

"Him...?"

He rose his head as it dawned upon him.

"You want me to raise the devil?"

Ava nodded.

"No. I can't do that."

Ava reached out her hand, sticking it into his chest and clutching his no-longer beating heart, squeezing it.

A stabbing pain soared throughout his body. His mind was filled with images of his family in tears. His wife stripped. His daughter whipped. His granddaughters ripped apart by teeth. His whole family raped and humiliated.

She withdrew her fist and looked at him.

"That will be your family's fate, should you refuse."

"I —"

"The devil will rise either way. This is the only way your family will be safe from him."

He bowed his head. Help the devil rise and protect his family.

He agreed to do it.

He was ashamed.

25

Kelly's mind filled with mist, fogging any sense of clear thought, or understanding. She held Eddie's hands firmly in hers, a sympathetically desperate look on her face.

"The Devil's Three?"

"Yes. The wounded, the dead, and the prophet."

"And who could they be?"

Eddie sat back in his chair and shrugged his shoulders, looking around the room anxiously. He had contemplated it so much that his mind was beginning to hurt. Kelly could see that. She could see the confusion etched over his face; his distant look, the twitching of his mouth in frustration, the leg that bounced up and down in agitation, even his hands that Eddie retracted from hers to clutch the side of his seat.

"Could I be, I don't know… the wounded?"

"I don't think so. It just doesn't feel right."

"Well, you could say you're the prophet."

"No. I would imagine I'd be the catalyst. They would want to bring forth the devil to unleash me, so I couldn't be part of the ceremony itself. I would be… What the ceremony is for."

Kelly bit her lip. She was only trying to help, and he was being dismissive. She did her best to understand, to realise he had been at this a lot longer than she had. It was so unfair that either of them had to have these burdens.

It was all unfair. Every bit of it.

"And you think they want to do it here? In this house?"

"What is with all of these bloody questions?" Eddie snapped, turning away. In the same breath, he stood up and marched upstairs, the heavy stomps of his feet resounding throughout the house, ending with the slamming of their bedroom door.

Maybe she could take a step back a bit. Let him think. Give him the time and space to figure it out.

But then again, how could she, when she too was being attacked?

Maybe that was why he was so frustrated, because he knew how much it affected her too, and he couldn't deal with the guilt…

These thoughts spun and spun into a web that blew apart in her mind. So many strands, so many possibilities, so much to consider.

I need to cut him a break. Support him.

She stood up, took a glass from beside the sink and filled it with water. Once she had drunk it, she placed the glass in the sink and followed Eddie's path upstairs.

As she approached the bedroom, she saw the door ajar. She grew cautious. She wasn't sure why she was slowing down and edging toward the door, there was just something about it. Something unclear that filled her with dread.

She creaked open the door, revealing Eddie stood beside the window with his back to her.

"Eddie?" she asked, so quietly she could barely

hear herself. In a way, she didn't want him to respond. Didn't want him to answer. She wasn't sure why, there was just something bad in the air.

She placed one foot carefully in front of the other until she reached him, placing a hand on his arm.

He didn't move.

"Eddie?"

"Kelly. I…" he began, and trailed off.

She tucked her arms around his waist, holding him closely.

"I know."

He turned around and took a firm hold of her face with his hands. She remained motionless, staring up at him

His eyes… they were strange. Different. They felt aggressively demanding.

It was a look she hadn't seen before.

Without any warning, his lips forced themselves into hers

She was taken aback at first. How could her kiss her so passionately at a time like this?

Then again, why shouldn't he?

Maybe it's what they needed?

He pushed his mouth harder and harder against hers. She reciprocated, despite feeling a little intimidated. He was kissing her hard, harder than passion requires, and it was making her lips hurt. She practically choked on his tongue as he slipped it into her mouth.

Peeling himself away, he hurled his top off and threw her onto the bed.

This is what we need. I know it, she decided. And she was right. It had been a while.

Before she could even think about objecting, he was on top of her, peeling off her clothes. As she went to kiss him more tenderly, eager to bring a sense of romance to the occasion, he grabbed her by the neck and turned her over.

For a few moments, all she could feel was his fist on the back of her head, pressing into the hair. He was pulling it. It hurt.

She struggled to breathe, her face choking into the pillow.

She made a weak attempt at thrashing her hands, but then she stopped as she felt him inside of her.

He was rough and it hurt. She was dry, but he had forced himself inside her without taking a second to think about whether or not she wished to partake.

She managed to peel her face away from the pressure against the pillow and put her weight onto her forehead.

She could finally breathe again.

She watched him, upside down, behind her. The smell of his sweat turned her on.

Just as she began to enjoy it, even feel him inside her in a pleasant way, he got even rougher.

He was pulling back and thrusting himself inside of her with such pounding frequency that she gave out a yelp. She tried objecting, but it turned into a whimper that went unnoticed.

She was merely his doll. His way of feeling better. He didn't care about her.

Was this even okay? Had she even given her consent? Did she need to?

She felt a trickle of blood slide down her inner thigh and decided it was time to stop.

She hit her arms out behind her, crying out,

"Eddie! Eddie!"

He took a hold of her arms and restrained them determinedly behind her back with one hand, and used the other to grab hold of her hair.

"Eddie, stop!"

Tears filled her eyes. She attempted to struggle out of his grasp, but it was no good.

She was bleeding harder. It was trickling down her legs.

She cried. He wasn't stopping, and there was nothing else she could do but cry.

He heatedly scraped her insides. Everything hurt. He was plunging himself into her too deeply, too hard, too quick.

She felt used.

"Eddie!"

The flashbacks of cows and sheep underneath her as she rode them played in her mind like a cinema screen.

She remembered how it felt.

She remembered how it hurt.

"Eddie, stop!"

Eddie froze.

She froze.

They stayed still, him inside her, but not moving. A few seconds later, she felt him take himself out of her.

She slumped onto her side, sobbing.

"Kelly?" Eddie knelt beside her.

"What do you want?" she cried out through her snarled teeth. He had never made her feel this pain before. She was physically, and emotionally, numb.

"Kelly." He took hold of her hand in his, but she

flinched it away.

"What?" she snarled again.

"Kelly, what just happened?"

She turned and looked at him, hostile, ready to snap.

His eyes were filled with tears. He looked feeble, emotional, distraught. This was not the face of the person who had just invasively assaulted her.

"Eddie?" she wept curiously.

"Kelly, I have no idea what just happened."

26

Anna sat alone, half silhouetted by the pale moon outside the window. Martin's heart ached, watching his mother appearing so solemn. She was all he had in the world, and he knew he had let her down.

"I got a call from your school today." She spoke slowly and quietly, which was strange, as he was so used to her getting angry and agitated over such little things. Instead, she just turned her head toward him, her face half-formed by the moonlight, her smudged tears glistening.

He edged toward her and pulled out a seat. Taking it slowly and particularly, he lifted his sad eyes to hers and forced a wounded smile.

He tried to take her hand in his, but she withdrew it.

"Thought you might," he nodded. He didn't bother with the light, they didn't need it. The room felt calm, but it also felt hopeless. Besides, the last thing he wanted was for her to see his injuries and get even more concerned, nor did they want to have to pay the electricity bill.

"You swore at a teacher. Walked out of school."

"I know, Ma."

"How do expect us to get by if we get fined?"

He didn't turn away. He didn't run, didn't flee

from the situation. Instead, he sat on the edge of his seat toward her, stroking his hand down her hair.

"I don't need school, Ma. I need to take care of you. What if you need the toilet during the day when I'm not here? They won't give us a full-time carer, you heard what they said."

"I don't give a damn what they said."

He paused, resting his arm around her shoulders.

The sight of his mother upset hurt him, and he struggled to hold in his tears. He told himself he was a man, and men didn't cry.

But she cried. Though she clearly did her best not to make any sound, her sobs were clear for him to see.

"In that case, I'll have to deal with myself, won't I?"

"But, Ma –"

"No! You listen to me, Martin. I want you to get an education."

"I don't care about no education."

She grabbed hold of his collar. He knew it would take everything she had to make such a strong, bold move. It would likely tire her out for the night, but she did it anyway.

"You will care," she spat through her choking tears. "Without an education, you'll end up the same way I did. Same way your father did. And I won't have that."

"Ma –"

"Because I love you."

He couldn't help it. He leaked tears. Man tears.

"I love you too, Ma."

He buried his head in her shoulder. He couldn't let her see him cry, nor could he bear to watch her fill with tears. It was too much.

He always wished for another life. But he never wished for another mum.

Finally, he pulled away, lifting his top and wiping his eyes. He held eye contact with her, forcing a smile, his heart breaking from the hurt look in her eyes.

She had never wanted to force this life on him. She knew the burden she placed on him. This accident was never her choice.

"Let's take you to bed, Ma."

He helped her out of the wheelchair and picked her up in his arms. She might have been able to make it half the way on her crutches, but it would be too much to ask.

As he tucked her into bed and kissed her on the forehead good night, he thought about what it would be like if she could do that to him.

If she could be the one lovingly putting him to bed. Like she did when he was little.

As he returned to the kitchen, he poured himself a glass of water into a dirty glass, flinching at the rancid taste. Then something caught his eye. Something glistening across the room. Something on his mum's wheelchair.

Pouring away the rest of the foul water, he dropped the glass into the sink and made his way over. He turned the wheelchair into the light and ran his hands over the writing.

There were some words written across the back of her chair. In gold. There was writing, in gold.

He did his best to make out what was written, but he was fairly sure it wasn't English. He wasn't sure what it was. It looked old, not some language he had heard.

Finding a receipt for something down the back of his trousers, he reached for a blunt pencil that lay on the kitchen side and wrote down the letters he saw before him. He held the piece of paper up to the light and scrunched his face up to try and make out what it was.

Surge, diabolum

He shook his head. Maybe if he had paid attention in school, he could…

Nah. This ain't English. No way.

He had done French at school, but it didn't seem anything like that either.

And where did she get the pen from? We barely own a pen, never mind a gold pen.

He reached around the bottom of the wheelchair, feeling over the wheels, not entirely sure what it was he was expecting to find.

He scanned the kitchen and the lounge area. He reached under the sofa cushions, under the seats, in the kitchen drawers. Nothing.

Then he saw it. Reflecting in the light. Up above himself, on top of the kitchen cupboards.

A gold pen.

He couldn't reach it. He had to hold out a chair to climb up and get it. But, sure enough, there it was.

On top of the kitchen cupboard.

Somewhere he couldn't reach without climbing on a chair.

His eyes fixated on it. A mind full of confusion.

How did she get a gold pen up here?

As hard as he tried to sleep that night, he couldn't. The words and the pen spun round and round his mind until it made even less sense than before.

27

23 July 2002

Kelly enjoyed the first dreamless sleep she'd had in a very long time. She was at peace, blankness in her mind; no flashbacks, no images, no violence. Nothing.

Until her eyes opened with a start. From a deep sleep to wide awake, in seconds.

Turning over to see the alarm clock, she gasped. It was 3.00 a.m. Exactly.

Eddie had told her the significance of this time. He had warned her of the dangers of this house, and the significance in the world of the paranormal.

She turned to check if he was awake.

He wasn't there.

Leaning up, she switched on a lamp and looked around the room.

Nothing. No one.

The door was ajar, a neat pool of moonlight leaking through the curtains. She placed her feet on the floor, feeling the carpet sink beneath her, gazing around herself. She crept forward, toward the door, and looked out into the hallway.

"Eddie?" she whispered.

Silence.

The door softly creaked as she opened it further, looking back and forth across the landing. There was no movement, no sound, just a still full moon boasting through the window.

"Eddie?" she spoke, this time a little louder.

No answer.

She left the room behind her, making her way across the landing and to the top of the stairs. As she took each step slowly and surely, she felt a draft upon her legs. She felt suddenly cold in just her pyjama t-shirt and shorts, a cold that reminded her of winter.

"Eddie?"

As she paused on the bottom step, she looked back and forth.

The backdoor was open. Through the kitchen. That's where the draught was coming from.

"Eddie?"

Still no answer. But she could see something, some black outline, some movement of shadow outside.

Step by step, she moved slowly but surely toward the backdoor, keeping her gaze fixed, worried as to what might jump out.

Huddling her arms around herself for warmth, she stepped onto the paving slabs outside the house. They were icy-cold on the soles of her feet.

There Eddie stood. Swaying ever so slightly from side to side. His eyes were wide open, without blinking. He was transfixed.

It freaked her out. It was like nothing she had seen; he was, without doubt, asleep. Yet his eyes were wider than they ever were when he was awake. They looked painful, his pupils bloodshot, his eye-lids peeled open as if being pulled by an invisible hook.

His piercing eyes were fixed on something in front of him.

"Eddie, come back to –"

She was unable to finish that sentence. She gasped, and jumped back, recoiling in horror.

The shed door flapped open in the breeze, and each time it did, she saw the same familiar sight.

A cat's head. Nailed to the back of the shed. Blood dripping from the entrails that hung loosely beneath its chin. A pool of dark red lay on the floor below it.

It was exactly the same as before.

She put her hand on Eddie's arm, squeezing it.

"Eddie, please."

A shuffle came from the leaves across the garden.

She jumped, flattening herself against the wall of the house. Peering into the shadows across the garden, she moved behind Eddie, as if he would be able to defend her.

He was still catatonic.

The silhouette of a man rustled beneath the tree across the small patch of grass. It was hard to make out, but she had no doubt someone was there. Amongst the shadows of the night, the silhouette stood.

And it looked straight at her.

"Eddie, please wake up."

The door behind her slammed shut. She ran toward it, grabbing onto it, trying to pull it open, rip it open if she had to.

It wouldn't move.

She looked back to the silhouette. It stayed still.

But it was there.

She knew it was there.

"What do you want?" She tried to sound threatening, but her voice was etched with fear.

She looked to Eddie, who remained motionless, transfixed, then back to the figure, a stationary individual. Just standing. Watching.

"Eddie, please, please."

She shook him. Nothing. No reaction. He swayed, and that was all.

"Please!" she cried.

Eddie's face turned toward her and she yelped against the wall.

His pupils disappeared, replaced by white, the veins of his face sticking out like red string.

He turned, walked toward the kitchen door, and opened it seamlessly.

The damn door opened.

She jumped inside with him and thumped the door shut, locking it, keeping her eyes on the figure that did not move.

It still did not move.

She turned to Eddie, but it was too late. He was walking at a steady pace toward the stairs.

Her eyes turned back to the figure.

Her skin prickled, hairs stuck up on end, blood rushing through her veins.

She realised she was shaking.

She swept the curtains across in a sudden motion and turned on her heel, running up the stairs, back across the landing and into the room, slamming the door behind her.

Eddie was in bed. Asleep. Snoring. Motionless.

"Eddie?" she asked.

His eyes slowly blinked open and he lifted his head.

"Kelly?" he asked, full of concern. "What are you doing?"

Her breathing accelerated, her senses heightened, keeping distance between her and him.

"Eddie?"

"Kelly, what are you doing?" He spoke as if nothing happened. "Come back to bed."

"I…" She didn't know what to say. "I will."

That was good enough for him. He lay his head back down on the pillow and fell back asleep.

She didn't move. She was stuck against the door.

Watching him.

Waiting for something. Waiting for nothing.

She woke up next morning, huddled in the corner of the room.

Eddie was still fast asleep.

28

Jenny was astounded at the sight of Eddie. Bags sat prominently under his eyes, which were creepily bloodshot. Each of his movements seemed sluggish. Even the simple act of lifting his latte to his mouth showed he was exhausted.

"Jesus, Eddie," she exclaimed. "I'm really worried about you."

He shook his head into the shortbread that sat solitary on his plate.

"I'm not getting much sleep," he admitted. "Neither's Kelly, to be honest."

"I hope you're both getting on okay. She's perfect for you. I know I said it when you got together, but…"

She faded off, recognising in her best friend's eyes that this was not relationship problems. This was something more.

"I'm scared, Jen."

He lifted his face and exposed his solemn eyes. They were full of emotion, riddled with doubt. They looked like they were permanently on the brink of crying and it broke her heart to see him this way.

After all they had done for each other.

She couldn't even remember her life without Eddie. He was too important to let dwell on this.

"Scared of what, Eddie?"

"I don't know…" He recoiled, his head sinking back to his beverage.

"Whatever it is, Eddie, you have taken on the depths of hell, the devil himself. Whatever it is, you can deal."

"That's the thing, you see." He shook his head and peered at the corner of the room, gathering his thoughts. He took a sip of his latte, not really tasting it, just biding time he could take to think. "I don't think it was that simple."

"Simple?"

It had been anything but.

She'd had to practically kill him, then stress as she helplessly watched Lacy revive him. She'd had to send him to hell so she could pull him back. It had not been simple.

"I don't mean what you did, which took so much courage. You were so brave."

Jenny blushed.

"Thing is," he continued. "I did that fireball thing at the devil and we made it out. It… It was just too easy. It's the ruler of hell, and it was just too easy."

He exhaled a breath of exasperation and leant back in his chair.

"What is this really about?" Jenny put her hand on his. "This can't be about what was a tremendous victory."

"It's just… things are happening again. And it's Kelly. I'm worried about her."

"Why?"

"She keeps having flashbacks. And I know they are terrible and I know she can't say these things out loud, it's just…"

His eyes welled up and he stifled back tears.

"Just what, Eddie?"

She smiled at him, gripping his hand in hers, showing him she was there.

"She can't talk to me about it. And now things are happening. Dead animals turning up at our house."

"Dead animals?"

"Yes. And there's this thing called The Devil's Three."

"The Devil's Three?"

"And these powers I have, they can't fight it, because they come from it, and –"

He stopped, choking on his words. They were in public, and if anyone overheard they would think he was crazy.

"Eddie, I don't know about any devil or three or dead animals… But I'll tell you what I do know."

Eddie turned his head away in denial, but she would not let it go. She grabbed his head and forced him to face her, looking dead into those painful eyes.

"You are the best person I know. The things you can do are incredible. Whatever it is, whatever you are up about, you will face it. And you will win."

"But what if I'm not a good person –"

"You are. You just need to believe it."

He nodded, sighing. Maybe she was right.

But how could she be?

Someone was putting these carcasses around the house. What if it was Kelly?

What if it was him?

What if it was neither of them?

What if it was –

Enough.

"Thanks, Jenny. I love Kelly so much, it's taken me so long to find her, I…"

He shook his head. He couldn't finish the sentence. It was too hard. The whole bloody thing was too hard.

"I know, Eddie. I know."

29

The wind was harsh and the clouds were grey as Kelly arrived at her front door.

She glanced over her shoulder. All day, she'd had the strangest feeling she was being watched. When she'd picked up her morning coffee, when she left her lectures, when she walked across the car park, she had felt it. An ominous feeling that rose through the pit of her stomach, filling her with alarm.

She couldn't see anyone. The bushes bustled, but that was mainly due to the unwelcome summer breeze. The sound of a loud television came from the house opposite, a car drove past... all fuelling her paranoia, but nothing particularly untoward.

But still, that feeling, it hung over her like an ensuing rain cloud waiting to pour.

After she let herself into the house, she locked the front door and placed the chain across, ensuring she was safely secured inside.

Dropping her bag next to her shoes and trudging through the hallway to the kitchen, she put the kettle on and slumped in a chair.

She was tired; these sleepless nights were finally getting to her. She had struggled to stay awake in lectures, even finding her eyes closing a few times. Honestly, if you were to ask what the lectures had been about, she wasn't entirely sure she'd have an answer. As her eyes rested, waiting for the kettle to boil, they felt warm and comfortable as her eye-lids met.

Knock, knock, knock.

Three resounding, solid knocks banged against the front door and echoed throughout the house.

Her eyes flung wide open with alarm. She stood. Should she call Eddie? The police? Should she run out the back door?

Then it dawned on her; why? It was perfectly normal for someone to knock on the door. It may be the postman, or a neighbour. Why was she so quick to plan her defence against a predator that may not even be there?

"You need to get a grip, Kelly," she told herself.

Still, as she edged toward the door, that ominous feeling spread through her gut once more. She'd had it all day, and this was only exacerbating it.

Knock knock knock.

"Okay, okay."

She removed the chain, undid the main lock, went to open the door – and froze.

If I needed it, I could get back to the kitchen and grab the knife from the drawer.

She wasn't entirely sure why she was needing an escape strategy. The feeling was just not going away.

As she opened the door, that feeling of dread changed to one of perturbed surprise. She did not recognise the man standing before her. He was not a neighbour, not someone she knew, and he was definitely not a postman.

Yet he seemed calm, pleasant even. Like he wouldn't harm a fly.

"Hello, I presume you are Kelly?" he asked, with a thick South African accent.

"Yes…"

He smiled a warm, genuine smile. He skin was a prominent black, and he wore some sort of multi-coloured robe. She was sure it was traditional South African dress; she may have even heard it called a 'venda' or something once, she wasn't entirely sure. Underneath that, he seemed to be wearing a polo shirt and jeans.

"My name is Bandile Thato," he introduced himself, grinning warmly in a way that made him instantly likeable. She loved his accent, and the way it made every syllable sound interesting. "I am looking for Edward King?"

"Er, Eddie isn't here at the moment."

"It is of the utmost importance I speak to him. Do you know if he will be back soon?"

"Well, yeah, any minute."

"May I come in and wait for him?"

Even with the friendliness and warm sensibility he introduced himself with, she still had that feeling in the pit of her stomach that made her hesitant to let a stranger into her home. Still, he had not given her reason to be suspicious, and the name Bandile Thato seemed familiar; like it was something Derek had once mentioned.

"Of course," she spoke eventually, after the silence had become awkward. She opened the door, allowing him into the house, shutting it behind him.

"I had just put the kettle on, would you like a cup of tea?"

"That would be lovely, thank you."

She led him into the kitchen.

"Please, take a seat."

He smiled at her once more, showing sincere gratitude. "You have a lovely home," he told her.

She poured the drinks and placed his in front of him, the whole time leaning herself against the cutlery drawer where she knew the knife was.

"So how do you know Eddie?"

"Ah, no, I just… I know of him. I have heard great things about him."

"Great things?"

"I know he has become a most powerful exorcist, one to rival anyone I have ever met. Word travels fast, even in another continent."

They did not have to wait long. After around ten minutes of small talk, the front door opened and Eddie strolled in.

When Eddie saw Bandile, he froze.

"Edward?" Bandile raised his eyebrows and smiled toward him.

Eddie nodded.

"My name is Bandile, and I have some news about Derek."

30

Despite approaching 8.00 p.m., the dark-orange sun still cast a dim light over the peaceful evening. The bushes outside the window were still, the street was empty and the lack of anything happening was almost unsettling.

Staring out the window was almost all Martin could do. They did not have enough money to top up the electricity, so he couldn't watch telly. There were a few tattered books on the floor behind the telly, but they weren't really his thing. He was bored, with nothing to do, but at the same time, he was also content. Happy just to sit still and embrace the silence.

His mother was asleep in her wheelchair next to him, having her 'early evening' nap. He honestly didn't get how she could sleep so much. He tossed and turned every night, often spending hours willing himself just to get some sleep that he knew would never come. Not her. She slept so soundly.

I suppose just living must be exhausting when you get out of breath from a few steps.

He wondered how long she would live for. Surely in the condition she was in, her life expectancy was limited. Even more than that, what would he do without her? What would be the purpose to his life then?

How would he even motivate himself to get out of bed in the morning, if he was all that was left?

Deciding it wasn't good for him to sit still and allow poisonous thoughts to stew around his mind, he stood up and paced around the room, stuffing a few cushions and picking up a few mugs, taking them into the kitchen.

He took a dirty glass and rinsed it out, then filled it with water. He felt the water fall down his dry throat and hydrate him, drinking nearly the whole pint glass in one. He hadn't realised he was that thirsty.

Clang!

His head shot around immediately.

A noise. It was something moving, something hitting something.

Without hesitation, he darted through to the living room to see what state his mum was in; but she was in the exact same position she had been in before. Fast asleep, her head slumped on her left shoulder, snoring away.

Scanning the room, he saw no obvious movement.

Shaking his head to himself and deciding he must have been hearing things, he walked back into the kitchen and refilled his glass.

He downed another half a pint and placed the glass on the side. He opened the drawers, searching for something to eat. There was a half-full jar of jam and an almost empty box of cereal that had only the crumbs left in the bottom from its previous use.

"Martin?"

His head shot around.

His mum's voice. Clear as day. Calling him from the other room.

Her voice was curious, rather than helpless, as if she had a question to ask.

He edged toward the living room, peering around the doorway.

She lay still, in her wheelchair, head rested on her left shoulder, snoring audibly. She had not moved. Nor had she awoken.

His eyes remain on her. Maybe she was talking in her sleep? Wouldn't be the first time.

But the tone of the voice was just… not in keeping with the way his mum talked. She whined, commanded, never enquired.

Shaking his head again, he turned around to leave the room once more.

That's when he heard it again.

"Martin?"

He shot around in an instant, absolutely one hundred percent sure his mum had just said his name.

"Ma?" he offered.

Nothing.

No reaction. She sat still. No movement. Just snoring.

He knelt beside her and stroked his hand down the side of her face. She felt warm, almost burning up; which was strange, as the house had an odd chill in it. Was she getting ill?

"Ma, you say something?" he asked again. No response. Just snoring.

He stood up and went to leave once more.

"*Maaaartiiiiiin!*"

This time it was an aggressive moan, an exclamation of sheer agitation, anger, abhorrence.

He darted to her side and took her face in his

hands, peering at her intently, adamant he was not hearing things.

Her snoring stopped. Her eyes didn't flicker. Her head didn't move. But her breathing was lighter.

"Ma?"

Her eyes shot open, sending him flailing onto his back in terror. The black of her pupils were fully dilated, growing to an inhuman size, like night between eyelids.

Her mouth opened and a piercing scream filled the house. Martin clutched his hand over his ears. It did not stop.

Another scream resounded, a mix of a lower-pitched growl accompanied by the high-pitched wailing, combining into a louder combination of screams.

Another few screams protruded from her wide-open mouth, a number of voices combining.

"Ma!" Martin screamed out, both petrified and horrifyingly concerned.

How the hell is this happening?

The scream stopped. As if it was the eye of the storm, she sat still.

Still Martin didn't move. Not yet.

Her chest lifted into the air. She rose with it, the rest of her body trailing upwards like the arms of a rag doll. As she levitated inches above her chair, she vibrated, seizing uncontrollably.

Martin couldn't believe what he was seeing. He questioned his eyes, adamant this couldn't be happening. She was still so close to the chair, maybe she wasn't flying, maybe she was just propped up, her chest spasming.

He knew it was denial. He knew what he saw.

Her head slowly lifted above her chest, freakishly slowly, the rest of her body still hanging helplessly. She focussed her dead, black eyes on Martin and grinned sadistically.

"You're going to die."

With that, she fell back into the chair, slumped down and continued snoring.

It was hours until Martin felt it was safe to move.

31

Eddie set a cup of tea beside Bandile and sat on the edge of a chair he had brought in from the kitchen. Kelly was sitting back in the armchair, deep in thought, staring at Bandile with wary scepticism etched all over her face. Bandile sat back on the sofa, his large body spread out, a warm grin on his face; not an annoying grin, but the kind of grin that indicates he is a kind person who looks for the good in others.

Eddie couldn't sit back on the sofa, nor could he slump into an armchair. He perched on the edge of the wooden chair, leaning toward Bandile, desperate for answers.

"It is lovely to meet you, Edward, after all this time," he spoke, his accent thick and endearing. "Derek has spoken so much about you."

Eddie nodded, urging him to get to the point.

"I don't know if you know, but I am the one who wrote the book of prophecies and gave it to Derek, in return for him freeing my wife from a demon, a long time ago." He looked to the corner of the room as if reliving the memory in his mind. "He did so well."

"And you said you know where he is?"

"Of course, you must realise, I never knew the prophecy would be about you. I apologise for what has happened. It is unfortunate."

Unfortunate?

Eddie bowed his head. He could feel Kelly watching him, almost as worried as he was. But he had a feeling there was more to the story than a simple identification of Derek's location.

"Tell me, Edward, have there been any strange occurrences happening?"

"You'll need to be a bit more specific, Bandile. I'm sure you know what line of work I'm in. Strange occurrences are everyday situations for us."

"Yes, I would imagine," Bandile nodded, smiling to himself. His smile faded as he leant forward slightly. "Have there been any dead animals around here, Eddie?"

Eddie shared a look with Kelly. He nodded.

"And what can you tell me?"

"Erm…" Eddie hesitated and took in a deep breath, considering whether he could trust this man.

Surely, he could. Derek had freed this man's wife, and this man had entrusted Derek with the biggest secrets of the future. He decided if anyone could be trusted, it must be Bandile.

"Well, yes," Eddie confirmed. "A dead cat's head, hanging in the shed."

"And did it have any writing next to it? In Latin, maybe?"

"Yes. Yes, we translated it, it said –"

"Rise, devil."

Eddie dropped his head and feebly nodded.

"Have you heard of The Devil's Three, Edward?"

"Vaguely."

"It requires a set of three people. One wounded,

one dead, and one a prophet. It is a ceremony undertaken with the sole purpose of rising the devil. I believe someone, somewhere, is planning to do this. And I think they are planning on using your house to do this, and these dead animals have something to do with it."

"Well then, we should go." Eddie and Kelly shared the same worried expression. "Get out of here."

"It would be no good." Bandile shook his head solemnly. "They will track you down and find you, there is no escape from them. If anything, it will waste energy you should be using otherwise."

"For what?"

"To resist."

"Resist what?"

Bandile sighed. Smiled sympathetically. There was clearly so much he knew that Eddie didn't.

"Do you know who you are, Edward?"

"The devil's link to this world, or something, yeah, I know."

"But I don't think you do. You are so much more to the devil than a link. He has plenty of links to this world."

Bandile rested his hand comfortingly on Eddie's arm, focussing him dead in the eyes.

"You see," he began, ensuring he was speaking clearly. "You are the antichrist. You are the coming of the devil in this world. Once he has risen from this ritual, once he is in this world, he will take that evil out of you. You will no longer be a man."

"Then I will fight him."

"The devil is the god of hell, you cannot fight a god. You don't seem to see it – once he has risen, he will bring out the evil that lays dormant in you, and you will be someone else. You will be *something* else. A demon. Of the highest order."

Eddie bowed his head. Kelly noticed him visibly upset, so she interjected with the questions she'd know he'd want answered.

"And these three," she softly spoke, "who are they?"

"I don't know."

"But you're a prophet. Could they intend to use you?"

Bandile looked down, then toward Kelly.

"I do not answer to the devil."

Bandile turned his head toward Eddie.

"You wanted to know what has happened to Derek."

Eddie's head rose. He was tired, fed up, done with everything; he had lived with this threat over his head for too long, and now he was being told it was coming to fruition. He thought he would be full of resistance and fight, but in truth, he was tired. Lethargic. He needed Derek's guidance, and without it, he felt like he was going to lose.

"Yes please. Tell me where he is."

"There was a plane crash. It happened when Derek was leaving Cambodia."

"Cambodia?"

"Derek was all over the world, searching for answers. Unfortunately, this plane went down, and…"

Eddie's eyes welled up.

"… and I'm sorry, Edward. I truly am."

Eddie covered his face with his hands. His stomach twisted, his gut entwined. His head filled with useless denial. He couldn't accept it. He couldn't.

"You're wrong. He can't have been."

Bandile smiled a sad, sympathetic smile.

Eddie stood and aimed for the kitchen, splashing hot water over his face.

It couldn't be true.

He couldn't face this without Derek. Not now. Not anymore.

Kelly appeared behind him, placing her hand on his back.

"I'm sorry, Eddie."

"I…" Eddie turned and whispered to her. "I don't believe him."

"Eddie, I – I've seen this man before."

Eddie looked at her peculiarly. He checked over his shoulder to make sure Bandile hadn't walked in, hadn't overheard them.

"What?" he asked.

"Last night, there was a figure in the garden, watching us. It was him."

Eddie turned wide-eyed, perplexed, not sure what to think.

"Think about it Eddie," Kelly whispered close to his ear. "He's a prophet. How could he not be able to predict a plane crash?"

"Do you think," Eddie glanced over his shoulder again, "do you think he's the prophet in The Devil's Three?"

"He *must* be lying."

"Edward."

Eddie shot around. Bandile stood in the kitchen behind him.

How the hell did he do that?

He had only just checked over his shoulder. How had he come in, unnoticed? Had he heard anything?

"Bandile?" Eddie asked, attempting to conceal his shaking hands.

"Is everything okay?"

Eddie nodded, then realised he was nodding frantically, so readjusted himself to a more casual nod.

"Everything's fine."

"I was just going to retire to my hotel room, if that is okay. I had a long journey, and I think you need time to process all this."

"I... I do."

"I will return tomorrow. Hopefully I will be able to answer more questions then."

Kelly's hand gripped Eddie's arm, and they barely moved until they heard the front door shut.

32

31 December 1993

Seven years before the millennium

Surrounding the pill packets and broken tissues, untouched glasses of water, defunct medicines, and useless self-help books, Bandile lay helplessly in his bed. It was a familiar bed, a bed he had become well accustomed to.

He could barely lift his hands. Such a young man, in his early 20s. The circumstances were "tragic," "sickening," "a real eye-opener," as all the people who met him would say.

Where were those people now?

Funny. Some of them had even labelled him "brave."

He was anything but. He hadn't chosen to fight this cancer. He hadn't chosen to have every part of him infected.

He hadn't chosen to die young.

These were all choices forced upon him. People

told him he should pray to God.

God?

Hah!

What had God ever done for him?

In that moment, he wished he had lived his life differently. Stayed faithful to his girlfriends, maybe even married one. What if he had pursued God with more vigour? Prayed for his redemption, his path to heaven?

He wasn't even sure if he believed in heaven anymore.

How could a god do this? How could someone so loving, so cherishing, commit such vile acts as to spread a cancer throughout the body of a man still discovering his place in this world? It was unfair.

Yes, it was not his predicament that was tragic, or sickening. It was God's. That bastard, who was responsible for the hell he had gone through.

Dying, without a faithful, loving human even by his side.

In his delirious state, he raised his fist to the air and attempted a "fuck you, God." His frail muscles barely managed the first syllable.

He was going to die. This was it. He felt it. His bones were weak and his muscles were heavy.

And there wasn't a damn soul around to care.

Except, in his delirious state, he saw something. Something he wasn't even sure was there.

A blurred figure. At the end of his bed.

Bandile attempted to lift his head, mustering his energy in an attempt to focus, make out who it was. Slowly, they came into clarity.

It was a young girl, no more than six, seven years old. Smiling at him. A long, black dress with a bow tied around her waist, a flower in her hair.

She swiftly glided around the bed to his side, stroking her warm hand down the side of his face. Her comforting smile made him feel content. Ready.

"Do I know you?" he spoke.

I can speak?

He hadn't been able to muster the energy to move his mouth, vibrate his vocal cords; now here he was, asking a fully formed question. The pain he was feeling slowly faded. He didn't understand.

"How can I speak? Am I dead?"

"You are not speaking." She smiled such a sweet smile. "But you are communicating with me. And no, you are not dead. Not yet."

Bandile was confused. He turned his head, manically looking around himself. The whole room had gone dark. It was like night had descended, and all that was left was a soft spotlight over him and this girl.

"I don't understand."

"I am a messenger. You see me in the form that would be most comforting to you, but this is not my true form. Not really."

"You mean, you're not a little girl?"

"No," she chuckled. "I am a demon wielding more power than you can imagine. This is just how you see me. It makes this whole process easier."

"What process?"

She looked him up and down, studying him with her eyes, taking in his condition.

"I represent the devil. I have come to offer you a deal."

"A deal? With the devil?"

"Yes."

"I don't believe in the devil."

"Well, he's going to offer you a deal whether you believe in him or not."

His head was fuzzy. He closed his eyes for a moment, opened them again, and this girl looked different. She had horns. Her dress exuded wavy flames.

Oh my God, she's on fire! She has horns! What…

"I have done this to show you that I am not of this world." The fires died down and the horns faded back into her head as she returned to the appearance of a little girl. "Now I expect you to listen to me, Bandile. This is a one-time offer."

"Okay…"

"The devil is willing to restore your life to you. He will remove every cancerous cell in your body. He will replace them with cells that will survive well into old age. What's more, he will bestow you a gift. A sight. You will be able to see the future."

"The future?"

"What's more, he will make you rich. You will be like a king to those around you. You will have more money than you could possibly imagine, and you will never have to work a day in your life. You will be surrounded by women, and people who love you. But you must do two more things in return."

Her sweet smile faded to a deluded, sadistic grin.

"He will send a woman to you possessed by a demon. You must track down a man called Derek Lansdale. From London. Ask him to exorcise this woman. In return, you will give him a book filled with all of the premonitions you have as a result of your new-found sight."

"Exorcise a demon? What?"

"Second condition. After the millennium, he will call on you once more. You must be part of a ritual, called The Devil's Three. You will act as the part of the ritual called the prophet, a label you will attain due to your powers. You must ensure this ritual is a success and that the devil rises. And you will ensure the heir to hell knows, so he can be brought forth."

"What?"

Bandile struggled to make sense of it all. So much senseless, deluded information. His thoughts were scattered, mixed into a vague haze.

"Do you want to live? Want to reach old age?"

"More than anything."

"Do you want to be rich? Be loved?"

"God, yes."

"Then you will ensure the devil rises. Do you understand?"

"What? I can't let the devil rise. I… What is going on…"

The little girl approached his side within a few sinister strides. Her eyes locked with him and, despite it being the face of the young and the innocent, he could feel that it was anything but.

"I have given you the terms for if you agree. I can give you the terms for if you don't."

"I –"

"Should you say no. Should you refuse." She pronounced the word 'refuse' with such venom, every syllable made him shake. "You will not only die from this cancer within seconds of my leaving, you will suffer. You will be ripped limb from limb, invaded, mutilated, raped, tortured, for an eternity in hell. Do you understand?"

"You can't do this…"

She held out a hand.

"Do we have a deal, Bandile Thato?"

He stared gormlessly at her hand. Then he thought no more of it. He nodded nervously, placing his hand in hers.

She clasped her hand firmly around his and shook.

In an instant, she was gone, and he was alone in his bed.

Only, he felt different. Renewed. Born again.

He had the energy of a young child.

And he couldn't help smiling.

33

24 July 2002

Two years, seven months since millennium

Her eyes shot open with a start. Abruptly leaning up, she turned her head to the alarm clock.

3.00 a.m. Again.

Get a grip, Kelly.

She slumped back onto the pillow, letting out an exasperated sigh. What she would give for a damn night's sleep. Not waking up at this bloody time for no good bloody reason.

She shut her eyes and thought about what life was like before. She had to really rack her brain to think that far back; before these flashbacks, before she was officially possessed, before she was committed to a psychiatric unit.

Back when she had two parents who cared and were just concerned about their daughter who having a few problems.

Back when they grounded her for a week for

shouting out at school, then telling a teacher to piss off when they told her to keep quiet.

But it was all for attention. It was a cry out, desperation for someone to listen to her, to help her with the chaos inside her mind.

Her parents hadn't seen it that way.

She barely spoke to them nowadays. Not because they'd had an argument, not because there was any hostility, not because it was a spoken agreement to distance themselves from each other; they had just naturally grown apart. Their lack of support, understanding, and care had meant she found new ways to cope. They spoke on the phone occasionally, but she couldn't remember the last time she had seen them. They hadn't even met Eddie.

Eddie had been so supportive. Ever since he had helped her, ridded her of the demon inside her. The support he had given her afterwards, all the time he had stayed by her side in the hospital; they had grown closer. And the first time they kissed it had just been a natural event, occurring after months of friendship.

She truly loved him. A real love, a love she couldn't fathom. Despite the difficulties they both faced, he was hers and she knew she could rely on him for anything.

Feeling a surge of warmth toward him, she turned in bed to put her arm around him and have a cuddle.

He wasn't there.

This sent shockwaves through her body. This time of night, Eddie disappearing from bed – its recurrence was cripplingly alarming.

She leant up and switched on the lamp. The bed next to her was empty. Her eyes darted around the room. Nothing.

She got out of bed and looked out of the bedroom window, into the garden. She saw him there, standing in front of the shed, staring gormlessly.

Again?

Concern consumed her. Something was going on. If Eddie saw this in someone else, he would recognise it as signs of possession, clear symptoms in need of an exorcism; if only he could see what he was doing, he would recognise his own need for help.

If only Derek was there, he would know what to do.

It must have been when he crossed over to save Derek, when he had faced the devil. Maybe it was time to stop denying, stop leaving things unsaid. It was time to confront the part of Eddie they had all wished wasn't there.

Better go get him back to bed.

She turned and headed for the bedroom door, opened it with an eagerness to help Eddie.

The last thing she saw before she was knocked out was Bandile's face.

Everything went blank after that.

"But evil men and imposters will proceed from bad to worse, deceiving and being deceived."

2 Tim 3:13

34

The high sun was overwhelming, its heat scorching the skin of dog walkers and happy families. Not a cloud was overhead, and a clear blue sky cast happy days upon happy people.

Eddie noticed none of this, for he was woken up by the horn of a car.

He promptly sat up and looked around.

Where am I?

He felt the gravel beneath his hands, the white lines marking in the middle of the surface, the curb of the pavement behind him.

He was in the middle of the road.

Standing up, he steadied himself, holding his hand to his head to cancel out his dizziness. Once his senses had returned, he noticed a man in a car before him honking his horn, accompanied by shouting and multiple obscene gestures.

Eddie waved his hand at him, grunting, "All right, all right," as he stumbled to the pavement.

Looking down at himself, he noticed he was topless, red pyjama trousers dangling off his waist.

How embarrassing…

Scanning the local area, he realised he was still in his estate; something he could at least be grateful for. He was around a two-minute walk from home.

How did I get here?

It had been a long time since he had sleepwalked this far. In fact, the last time he sleepwalked this much, he was being haunted by the demon Lamashtu. Not a particularly good omen to consider.

As he made his way back to his house, he gave a few nods at numerous neighbours walking their dogs or setting off to the shops, grateful for them just saying hi and not asking any further questions.

From how high the sun was in the sky, he assumed it was nearly midday. He wondered how no one had at least attempted to wake him up, or move him off the road. Saying that, they may well have, but were unable to wake him. They surely would have rung an ambulance or something, right?

He entered the house, rubbing his sinus, his head pounding.

"Kelly?" he shouted, then realised she would likely be at lectures. How come she hadn't tried to find him?

He assumed she must have thought he'd left before her and just gotten on with her day.

After drinking a glass of water with two ibuprofens in an attempt to cure his headache, he had a quick shower. He was lucky that he only had afternoon classes on this day, otherwise he would have had some awkward explaining to do.

Once he had showered, he dressed in his clean black shirt, red tie, and blue suit, put a little wax in his hair and brushed his teeth.

Before he left, he paused, peering around the bedroom. The bed was unmade, which was unusual. Kelly hated the bed being unmade, it was one of her pet hates; many a time he had learnt the hard way to ensure it was made when he got up later than her.

Deciding she may have woken up late and hurried into work, he did it for her, tucking each corner neatly underneath the mattress.

He glanced once more at the room before he left, noticing her clothes she had laid out for the day still spread over the chair.

His brow furrowed and he paused to think on this. It was really strange. But she could have just decided on something else to wear. Surely? She could have changed her mind.

He noticed the time and realised he was going to be late for his afternoon class if he dwelled on this any longer. Deciding there was likely a rational explanation, he grabbed his car keys and left for work.

35

Despite the crushing heat, Martin still felt cold. He wrapped his jacket around himself, huddling it close for warmth. In front of him was the local university. A hive of education and learning, students older than him, buzzing with the power of learning.

It was a place he would never be able to attend. Education had never been for him. But it may hold the man who could give him answers.

He had searched the local library top to bottom for answers, attempting to read all the books on the paranormal or the supernatural. Most were either written by nut jobs speculating about how because something not even the slightest bit spooky happened to them, it must be a sure sign of a ghost. The rest, the few books that seemed to have some integrity to them, were written in complex English he had to keep reading again and again to even get a slight understanding as to what they were on about. He was sure they had some kind of indication where he could find answers, but with words like 'confounding' 'arbutuses' and 'substantial,' he had struggled to comprehend them. It was at that point he wished he had paid a little bit more attention in school, and scoffed at the irony of it.

Eventually, he had found it in the newspaper

archives. An article about the local university opening a Paranormal Studies Department around a decade ago. It was setup by a guy called Derek Lansdale, and had made loads of progress with some exorcist guy called 'Edward King.' The newspaper reporter had been interested yet sceptical, but he was sure if they had a whole university department dedicated to it, they must have some idea what was going on.

Maybe if he could find these guys, they could tell him why his ma's eyes turned black and she floated up in the air.

Unless he was going crazy.

Which is far more likely.

He came to reception and waited behind a few students who were discussing a deadline or something with the lady behind the desk. They spoke with long words and well-spoken accents. He hadn't felt so out of place before in his life.

But if it meant helping his ma, he had to do it.

Finally, they left, and he took his place in front of the desk. The lady, middle-aged, with curly hair and a pair of glasses propped so far down her noise it must be counterproductive to her wearing them, sneered at him with judgemental eyes. He could tell she was sizing him up, wondering why some teenage misfit has come to the university.

"Can I help you?" She spoke with that snooty posh voice the others were using.

"I'm looking for the Paranormal Department."

"Do you have an appointment?"

He sighed. He just needed directions, not a lecture.

"Yeah. Meeting Derek Lansdale at half four."

"Derek Lansdale is out of the country."

"Oh, right. Yeah, I meant Edward King. Sorry."

He peered at her hopefully, praying she didn't see through his bullshit.

"Down the hall, follow the signs to the Psychology Department, then to Parapsychology."

"Cheers."

He turned and walked down the corridor. It was tidy, neat, with various signs to places like "Lecture Room 1" and "Meeting Room 3." In the windows of various rooms he could see young adults sitting attentively to a discussion with older adults, normally with a wise beard and glasses or something.

I so do not belong here.

He made it to the Parapsychology Department and found a lecture theatre. He turned the door handle slowly and peered in, rotating his head back and forth, surveying the vacant room. There were rows and rows of seats, a large screen, and an open space at the front. Spotting an office across the room, he walked over and knocked on the door.

"Enter," he heard a voice speak from inside.

As he entered, a man, far younger than he was expecting, held up his hand as he continued a conversation on the phone.

"Yeah, and you haven't seen her?" this guy was saying. "Did she attend your lecture? Well, look on the register. What do you mean, you didn't take one; how did you not take one? … Right, yes please, find out and let me know as soon as you do."

He hung up and turned to Martin.

"I apologise, just trying to track someone down. How can I help you?"

"Are you Edward King?"

"Yes." Eddie looked at him peculiarly. "Yes, I am."

"My name's Martin. I need your help."

"How old are you, Martin?"

Martin paused. He considered whether to lie. Then he figured that if this guy was going to give him any help, he would need to be upfront with him straight away.

"I'm fifteen," Martin grunted honestly, watching Eddie for his vague reaction.

"Okay," Eddie smiled. "Have a seat. And don't call me Edward. It's Eddie." Martin smiled thankfully and took a seat opposite him.

"So, what can I do for you?"

"It's my ma," Martin confided. "She... Something's happening to her."

"And have you tried talking to doctors?"

"Yes. Well... not about this. I mean, she's disabled. In a wheelchair. She was in a car crash, I take care of her."

"I'm sorry to hear that, Martin."

Martin smiled. No one had ever said that to him before. He wasn't sure why, but it made him feel both warm and sad. Such a caring statement, so easily given yet not given enough.

"But, I mean, some weird stuff's been going off, I can't explain it."

"I know first instinct can be to look at the abnormal, but most of the time these things are normal. Has anybody seen her regarding a mental health diagnosis?"

'Regarding'? 'Diagnosis'? It took him a few seconds to understand what Eddie was going on about.

"It's not that. She isn't capable of walking more

than two steps without needing to sit back down. She can't even go to the toilet herself. And she's doing stuff that not even she can do."

"Why don't you start from the beginning, Martin?"

And so he did. He told him about the other night, the levitation, the eyes, the saying his name. He admitted how much it freaked him out, how scared he was, how much she was the only thing in his life keeping him going.

"And was this the first time anything has happened?"

"Nah. The other day I came back and found somethin' written on her wheelchair, behind her back. But it was in some kind of weird language or somethin'."

"What did it say?"

"I don't know how to say it."

"Could you write it down?"

He nodded, and Eddie produced a notepad and a pen. Martin wrote down carefully:

Surge, diabolum

Eddie stared at it. Didn't talk, didn't move, didn't even blink. Martin felt a bit freaked out, not understanding what was going on. Eddie didn't move whatsoever. He looked like someone had just put a gun to his face.

"What is it?" Martin asked eventually, feeling increasingly awkward.

"Where did you say this was written?" Eddie asked in a whisper, choking on his words, barely about to string his sentence together.

"It was written behind my ma's back on the wheelchair."

Eddie ran his hand through his hair and stroked his chin, the whole time his eyes not removing themselves from those two words.

The exact same words that Eddie had found written on the wall of the shed.

"Do you, like, know what it is?" Martin wondered.

"It's Latin. I've seen it before."

"What does it mean?"

"It mean's 'rise, devil.'"

Martin understood why Eddie had reacted this way. Why the hell had that been written on his ma's wheelchair?

"Martin, write down your address for me," he instructed, his eyes still not moving. "I will be around as soon as I finish here, to see your mother."

"Is she okay?"

Eddie didn't answer.

36

There was a faint dripping coming from somewhere Bandile couldn't detect. The cold moisture hung in the air and on his tongue. Every footstep echoed against the bricks. The floor was hard, leaving remnants of grey dust over his feet, and the corners were occupied by a multitude of spiders; some dead, some alive.

It was a small room about the size of a garage, somewhere underground, the address of which had been delivered to him by that familiar face he had seen so many years ago. The confined space made him feel nervous, but he was assured in the task he had to do and did it with full confidence.

He had given up fighting it many years ago.

He hated himself. No, more than hated... He loathed himself. He *detested* his actions.

For a moment, he even felt sorry for the difficult choice he had been forced to make, then abruptly realised he did not deserve such things as sympathy.

For almost ten years he had been filthy rich. Everything he had ever wanted was there. Women. Money. Respect.

Life.

A life that was so almost taken from him through a

sickening cancer spreading so fast through his body it had been almost undetectable. A cancer that was gone in seconds, replaced by an endless supply of mansions, cars, friends, riches.

Oh, he had taken his side of the deal all right.

Now it had come time for him to meet the requirements he had to fill for the life he had undeservedly attained – or face an eternity in hell.

He had no choice.

But that didn't make it any easier.

Kelly's eyes were yet to open. But he was prepared. Ready for the screams, the protests, the begging for mercy. Ready to be defiant, ready to fulfil the task that was required of him.

He just had to force himself to realise – the devil would have risen with or without his help. His plans would have come to fruition whether he had taken the deal or not. Only carrying out these actions on the lord of hell's terms would have saved him from the eternity of suffering the rest of the world would face.

If it wasn't him doing this, it would have just been someone else.

Or so he told himself.

He finished securing her hands behind her back with handcuffs, her legs shackled to the wall via restraints around her ankles and a charring rope squeezed tightly around her chest and the chair, many loops holding her securely in place. She wouldn't be able to barely move.

He felt oddly proud of his work, despite the surgical removal of ethics he'd had to undergo to retain his mortality.

"This her?"

The voice from behind him made him jump. He

spun around in an instant circular motion.

"You scared me out of my skin!"

"Sorry," replied Jason Aslan, who stood weakly behind Bandile. "I don't really need to use a door or anything. The perks of being dead."

"Well, wear a bell next time, or at least cough."

Jason echoed Bandile's body language, hoping it would give him more confidence in the betrayal of humanity he was undertaking. Both of them took a strong posture with folded arms, glaring at Kelly bound unconscious before them.

Jason remembered her. It was the last face he had seen before he died. Right before her possessed body sliced his head off. Even though he knew it hadn't technically been her that had done it, he felt an odd sense of satisfaction at seeing her get her comeuppance.

If it wasn't for him being in that damn room, with those damn exorcists, with that damn girl, he would not be in this predicament. He would be alive. Surrounded by his beautiful grandchildren, his loving wife, and his adoring daughter.

If Edward King and Derek Lansdale hadn't involved him, he wouldn't be forcing these events on them. Despite not being particularly willing to undertake his tasks, he was vaguely pleased he was at least getting some revenge.

He had to hold onto that thought, that part of him that sought retribution. Otherwise the lack of morality his actions would need to endure would lead his family to an everlasting black pit of pain.

"So we're nearly there," Bandile observed. "Just one more to get."

Jason nodded.

Jason convinced himself this was the right choice.

He convinced himself this was the only choice.

Unknowingly, Jason and Bandile both stood there, sharing the same trail of thought. If the devil was going to rise, they wouldn't be able to stop it. They may as well save themselves.

"I don't really get it," Jason admitted. "So this Devil's Three, I mean, how exactly do we do it?"

"We need to sacrifice what we call the 'suffered.' This girl has suffered more than you could imagine. She was possessed by the devil. She will be an ample sacrifice."

"And... us?"

Bandile hesitated.

"We are close to having our Devil's Three. We have the prophet," he indicated himself, "and the dead," he indicated Jason.

"And who's going to be the wounded?"

Bandile took a loaf of bread out of his bag and ripped the end off with his teeth.

"Her name is Anna."

"Anna?"

"She's in a wheelchair. Only has a son. Shouldn't be able to put up much of a fight."

"Then we do the ritual and... and it's over?"

"It's over. And you can sail on up to heaven."

Jason lifted his head back and closed his eyes, imagining such an opportunity. He had been held in purgatory for so long. And he was so close. Just one more task, and that was it.

It wasn't long to go now.

37

This boy's house felt like a closet. Eddie could barely move without bumping into a wall or stepping on something left on the floor. The sink had a pile of dirty dishes, the wood on the cupboards was splintering, and rips of magazines, remains of crisps, and various bits of fluff were engrained into the carpet. There was something in the air that made his eyes water and a stench of something decaying that he couldn't quite place. This was a home of people who were struggling, and Eddie didn't feel disgusted; he felt sympathetic, and grateful for the life he had, despite the obvious predicaments he was facing.

Martin led Eddie through to the living room, where a small lady sat shrivelled up in a wheelchair. The room was colder, but he wasn't sure whether this was a sign of possession or because they couldn't afford to pay the heating. With the sun glaring through the windows, he made his mind up. There was something about this woman that left an unsettling, eerie, twisted feeling in his belly.

She needed his help.

But with what had been written on her wheelchair, he needed to be cautious. There may be a bigger reason he was there.

He knelt before her, looking her in the eyes. She

didn't move. Her face was slumped onto her shoulder, her eyes slanted to the side, staring at something beyond Eddie, without blinking.

"What's her name?" Eddie asked Martin, not quite sure why he was doing it in a whisper.

"Her name is Anna."

Eddie nodded.

"Hello, Anna. My name is Eddie. Can you hear me?"

Nothing. Not even a grunt, sigh, or snigger. Usually these things found his presence funny, at first. But she didn't.

"Anna, do you know who I am?"

He wasn't sure what he was expecting, but she stayed motionless.

He decided to try a different tact. Taking her hand in his, he used his other hand to turn her face toward him.

Anna's dead eyes now fixed upon his. Her mouth dropped open, trickling drool onto her chin and dripping onto her lap beneath her.

"Anna, I am here to help you."

"She's not normally like this," Martin gasped, Eddie able to hear tears in his voice. He didn't need to turn around to see that Martin was distraught. "She's usually complaining or going on at me about something. She isn't like this."

Eddie had seen this catatonic state before, usually before something screamed or the room shook. He remained wary, rubbing her hand affectionately, letting her know he was there.

"Okay, Anna. If you don't want to talk to me that's fine. What about anyone else? Is there anyone else in there who would like to talk?"

Her body didn't move, her eyes didn't move, her head didn't move; but Eddie detected the faintest movement in her mouth to represent a small but smug smile.

"Ah, yes. I see there is. And what is your name?"

The hand he was rubbing flinched. Its nails stuck into Eddie, slowly applying more and more pressure, until the nails were digging in hard, going further and further into his palm. As it started to cause him pain, he withdrew his hand and stroked his chin in thought.

"Surely you know who I am? If you are not Anna, if you are some beast dwelling within, you must know of me?"

Her head moved slightly up and down, maybe only a centimetre, in a slight but definite nod.

It knew. It knew who he was.

"And so, you know what I can do?"

Its mouth moved, a croaky breath exiting between her cracked lips, as if trying to say something.

"Do... you?" she muttered with a delicate vibration of her lips.

"Do I know what I'm capable of?"

Another one of these damn demons telling me I don't know what I've got inside of me.

"Why don't you tell me?"

He was frustrated, and he knew he shouldn't let it rattle him. He was just fed up. Fed up of not knowing what was inside of him. Fed up of not knowing how close The Devil's Three were to bringing out evil he kept concealed.

"You wrote something. Something in Latin, on the back of your chair. Do you remember what that was?"

She grinned a grin that didn't belong to her. Nodded a nod that was motivated by pure evil. So slight, such small movement, with such gleefully sinister intent.

He hated this thing, whatever it was.

"What's going on?" Martin was bouncing agitatedly from leg to leg, tossing his fist from palm to palm, breathing quickly with stress and terror.

Eddie stood and turned to him, holding his arm out to the tattered sofa beside them. Martin did as Eddie indicated, taking a seat, and Eddie knelt in front of him.

"You did the right thing in coming to me," Eddie told him. "There is something going on. Something more."

"What? What is it?"

"I think there may be a demonic force at work here, something within your mother's body, something latched onto her soul."

"What?" Martin screwed up his face and shook his head, disbelief etched over his expression.

"It's hard to take Martin, but demons, ghosts... the devil... they are all real. And I fight them every day."

"So get it out of her!"

Eddie sighed and stood, turning toward the window.

"It's not as simple as that." He turned back toward him. "What is going on with your mother is part of something much bigger. Part of a war I have been waging for a long time."

"What, how?"

"I believe –"

Anna spoke. What she said, neither of them could tell, but she said something in a loud grunt, followed by a deep, elongated cackle that sent dread through Eddie's blood.

"What did she say?" Martin yelped out.

Eddie knelt before her, showing his war face, his authoritative smirk.

"Would you like to repeat that?"

With a cackle, the thing before him complied.

"The suffered has been taken…" the deep voice practically sang.

Eddie stood.

The suffered has been taken?

Then it hit him like a bucket of icy-cold water in the face.

The Devil's Three. They needed 'the suffered' as a sacrifice.

And they have that sacrifice?

And that is when he realised.

Kelly.

38

Kelly's eyelids fluttered and slowly pried themselves apart, revealing a selection of dark blurs. She could see nothing.

The smell of humid moisture in the air hit her at first, followed by an overwhelming stink of decay. Something dripped, somewhere, far off, in an almost rhythmic, steady beat. Her head pounded, her failed vision making her dizzy.

She went to lift her hand to rub her head and found she couldn't. She struggled to move it once more. She felt steel clamped tightly around her wrists, pressurizing the bumps of her wrists with an awkward pain she dreaded to think she was going to have to continuously endure. Her arms were fixed to her body, bare skin of her forearm shredding dead flakes from the burning frays of old rope. Her ankles flapped about in fear, but only marginally, finding themselves restrained by cuffs that only allowed a fraction of movement.

Where am I? How did I get here?

She remembered in flashes.

Eddie outside.

The clock said 3.00 a.m.

She was fed up of not being able to sleep.

Bandile's face.

That was the last thing she remembered – Bandile's face.

Followed by a thud. The sound of a thud. The feel of carpet hitting her face. Then nothing.

Darkness. Complete darkness.

Then she was here. Her vision slowly returning, coming into focus.

The room was an empty darkness, a single light bulb hanging from the roof above her, giving a slight illumination that surrounded itself with shadows and black corners. The dust of the floor floated up and made her choke, the brick walls made any movement echo and the cold pierced through her skin.

She was wearing pyjamas. That was the next thing she noticed. She was still wearing her pyjamas. Whoever did this, it wasn't a sexual thing, otherwise she would not still be in those pyjamas.

Why am I thinking about fucking pyjamas?

A shuffle. A flicker of movement the opposite side of the light bulb. She squinted. Strained to see what it was, something in the distance, something coming toward her.

The solemn black face of Bandile presented itself with agonising smugness, filling Kelly with a vacant rage that welled up inside her, turning into nothing. She could do nothing. She couldn't even move.

"You're an arsehole." Not the cleverest thing she could say, but the most pertinent.

She felt weak.

A helpless damsel.

As if her position as a woman was being destroyed, an insult to the history of feminism; her being submissive before an overpowering, muscular man, holding her helplessly against her will.

"What do you want?" she decided was more productive.

She told herself not to panic. She willed herself to remain calm. Her mind told her to cry, told her to scream, told her to shout out for help. Her common sense told her it would be no good. This wasn't an impulsive abduction, this was planned. Shouting wouldn't be much good. She may as well save her voice.

"You're very lucky, Kelly," Bandile told her, that damn warm smile he constantly displayed on his face displaying itself once more – though this time, it wasn't so comforting. "You are going to be a sacrifice to a god. Not many people get chosen for such an act."

She nodded. It all made sense.

So I am 'the suffered.' Great.

"You think he's going to repay you for this?" Kelly shook her head.

"Why, whatever do you mean?"

"The devil is not a god, he is an angel fallen from heaven. God will win in the end."

"Is that what Edward told you? That good will win in the end?" He crouched down before her. "Does he think his good will win in the end? Because it won't."

"You don't know that."

"Oh, I do. This whole thing is for him. Once we have completed this ritual, the devil will bring forth who he is, what he is. He will no longer be the Edward King you know. He will not be able to return. He will be the antichrist personified, the evil representation, the eternal dictator of this world."

He laughed.

"You don't stand a chance," he told her.

"And what do you get?"

"Life. Money. He brought me back from the dead."

"Even he can't bring people back from the dead."

"Can't he?" came a voice from the back of the room.

A man walked forward. A man who appeared older than Bandile, with a beard, and weary eyes, and...

She knew him. She had seen his face in so many of her nightmares. Again and again and again.

She had chopped his head off.

"How...?"

"Hello, Kelly," Jason spoke softly. "I am sorry about this."

"You're sorry?"

"Yes."

He looked down, ashamed.

"Sorry enough to stop this happening? What the hell are you doing?"

"This is the only way to save my family from him, to save us from an eternity in hell."

"Or you could not do the ritual, then –"

"Shut up!" Jason cried, desperate not to hear it. "You don't know anything. You're a little girl. With no idea of true sacrifice."

He retreated into the far corner of the room, sank into shadow, and she could no longer see him.

"And Derek?" she aimed at Bandile. "What of Derek?"

"I'm afraid I wasn't lying there. Jason crashed his plane. He's dead."

"Did you see his body?"

Bandile smiled and dropped his head.

"You are such a prick," Kelly told him.

He reached out to a bag beside him and withdrew some duct tape. He pressed it against her mouth, then tied it around her head, bringing it around her mouth once more. He tied it around and around her head until she couldn't even breathe through her mouth, relying solely on her nose.

He slapped her face jokingly. "I'm tired of talking."

He turned toward the shadow Jason had disappeared into.

"I'm going to get the wounded. We complete the ritual at 3.00 a.m. Get her ready."

He took a ceremonial gown out of the bag and flung it on the floor beside his feet.

"A few hours and you will be free, Jason."

And with that, he disappeared into the darkness of the opposite side of the room.

A door open and shut, then bolted multiple times.

Kelly bowed her head and closed her eyes. Her body relaxed, but not from a release of the tension she felt; it was from the despair that spread throughout her. There was nothing she could do. There was no way she could protest, could fight, could even move.

By the time morning came, she would be dead.

Please, Eddie. Please.

She closed her eyes and prayed in her mind to a God that had done nothing to help them so far.

She would have to put her faith in the good in Eddie, that it would win. Without that faith, she was as good as dead.

The world would be as good as dead.

39

After fumbling his keys, his clumsy hands finally twisted the lock, and Eddie nearly barged the front door off its hinges. It slammed behind him as Eddie sprinted in, leaving it clattering against the wall.

"Kelly?" he shouted, pausing in the hallway, awaiting a response.

Silence.

He ran into the kitchen, his eyes darting around. His mug from that morning's cup of coffee hadn't even moved.

Kelly hated dirty mugs being left out. She became agitated with Eddie every time he left one out, putting it in the sink for him whilst ranting.

The cup hadn't been moved.

The cup sent chills running throughout Eddie's body.

"Kelly?!" He tried once more.

He stumbled forward, struggling to retain his balance, clambering into the living room and looking around.

Nothing.

He rushed to the stairs and ran up them, falling onto the floor of the landing and climbing back to his feet.

"Kelly?!"

He kicked the bathroom door open first, darting his eyes to every corner. He even shoved the shower curtain aside, ridiculing himself in his mind for it – did he really expect her to be waiting in the shower?

Through the hallway, he made his way to the bedroom, rushed in.

Nothing. Another bad sign.

He rushed to the spare room. It was empty.

Rushing back to the main bedroom, he ran to the window and looked out into the garden.

The trees were still, the grass was neat, the shed door hung open.

He accelerated down the stairs once more and fell, landing on his arm. He didn't care. He'd deal with the dead muscle later. For now, he needed to check the final place of the house he had not checked.

He rushed to the backdoor.

Praying she was there, hoping, wishing, desperately needing her to be there, he peeled the door open.

In his gut, he already knew the answer.

The garden had remained untouched.

The shed door was open. Vacant. An empty wooden box. The leaves of the bushes fluttered in the breeze and the open grass remained blank.

Shutting the door behind him, he made his way to the kitchen. Slowly. He had stopped rushing. This time he walked stiffly, absently unaware of where his legs were taking him.

The whole movement of walking slowed down to a meagre blur.

His feet fell like empty lead, weighed down yet floating forward.

His belly was vacantly sick. His head full of

nothing. His soul a hefty abyss.

His body slumped onto the chair, his eyes staring into nothing and not moving from that nothing. His arms propped out on the table, his breathing increasing, his heart racing. He felt himself unmovable. Frantically stationary. Triumphantly lost.

She was gone.

He couldn't think what to do next. This was the kind of situation where Derek would swoop in with some answer, casting an illumination of wisdom over the situation.

Except, Derek was not there. And if Bandile had been right, he would never be coming back. If what Bandile had said was –

Bandile…

It struck him like a sharp migraine. Where was he?

He had left the number of the hotel he was staying at. Kelly had written it down and left it…

He dashed to the kitchen side, where he found a ripped-out piece of notepaper with the number of a hotel. He took the phone off the wall and allowed his dead fingers to urgently dial it in.

Placing the phone to his ear, he found no surprise in what he heard.

"We are sorry, but the number you have dialled is incorrect."

He slammed the phone back against the wall.

Leaning against the kitchen side, he allowed a tear to fall.

But only a solitary tear.

He was distraught, but resolute. At least he had a clue, an inkling as to who might have taken her.

That's when his next realisation came. The Devil's Three… They had their sacrifice now, 'the suffered' –

which was Kelly.

They also required a prophet.

Bandile.

They also required the wounded. But who –

Fuck. No. You idiot, Eddie, you absolute idiot.

He knew who was next.

He knew who the wounded was.

Grabbing the car keys, he ran to the door.

In his gut, he knew it was already too late.

40

Martin slumped on the sofa, waiting impatiently. Eddie had said he'd be back soon, but he was taking his time. Why had he been so desperate to get out of there?

What was it about his mum that freaked him out so much?

Looking at his mum, he understood why she may perturb some people. She was making him increasingly uncomfortable. She had never been like this before; she had always been strange, irate, unfair even, but never had she sat like she was at that moment.

Her empty eyes rested on Martin. Her head was dropped down, slumped against her shoulder and her neck, without any movement, those eyes focussed on him. Those eyes looking up at him without movement, adamantly pinned.

But they weren't his ma's eyes. Ma's eyes were sometimes irritable, but usually warm.

These eyes looked sadistic. Brutally vulnerable.

Her breathing was the only sound that filled the room. Deep and croaky, like nails on a chalkboard. The smell of foul burning occupied the house, but there was no smoke. He had searched for the smoke everywhere, but to no avail.

He could even taste the contempt in the air, like a mixture of condensation and heat, forcing his tongue to boil.

This was not Ma. Ma was long gone.

Four thumping knocks resounded on the front door.

About time.

Martin left the room, keeping his eyes on Ma until the moment he had walked into the narrow doorway. He peeled the front door open and stood in stumped shock at what he saw.

"Hello," said a large, black man with a funny accent Martin couldn't pin. It wasn't British, but beyond that he couldn't tell.

"What?" Martin grunted. This wasn't the time for a cold call. Yet, this man didn't look like he was a cold caller. His had a large grin on his face, warm yet unsettling, as if he knew something Martin didn't.

"I'm here to help you with your mother," the man told him.

"Oh," Martin replied, wondering who he may be. "Are you with Eddie?"

"Sure…" the man replied, taking his time, clearly mulling something over in his mind. "Yes, I'm with Eddie. He sent me. May I come in?"

With a cautious look up and down the stranger, a narrow-eyed stare trying to suss this guy out, Martin stood back and allowed him in.

Wiping his feet on the welcome mat with thorough precision, the man took another step in, allowing Martin to close the door.

"May I wash my hands?" he asked.

"Sure," Martin replied, and nodded to the kitchen. He watched as the man walked into the kitchen and washed numerous times, ensuring the soap went through each of his fingers and over both sides of his hands.

After drying every part of skin on his hands with the manky towel left strewn over the kitchen side, he made his way back to Martin.

"That's better. May I see her?"

Martin nodded elusively, still staring at him. He had a nervous feeling about this overwhelmingly tall and muscular character, but trusting the fact he had said he was sent by Eddie, he led him into the living room where his ma was waiting.

The man's grin grew even bigger as soon as he feasted his eyes upon Anna, spreading right across his face, his eyes lighting up with pertinent joy and clear jubilation.

"Lovely," he acknowledged.

"Lovely?" Martin repeated, confused. "Mate, this ain't lovely. Eddie said she was possessed or somethin'."

"Yes. She is. Terribly possessed. I will need to take her away right away."

"Take her away?" Martin's voice rose, his temper growing irate. "Eddie said nothin' 'bout takin' her away. What you on about?"

The man turned his face toward Martin and tightened his lips, as if entering deep thought, attempting to decide on a difficult conclusion.

"Who are you?" Martin demanded. "What's your name?"

"My name is Bandile. Ask Eddie, he knows me, he will tell you."

"Right, well, she ain't goin' nowhere till Eddie gets back. He said 'e'd be back, an' we'll wait till then."

Bandile chuckled.

Martin's blood surged.He grew furious.

This guy was laughing? His ma was in this shitty state, and this guy was having a joyous moment over it? Who did he think he was?

"Fuck you laughin' 'bout, mate?" Martin squared up to him.

Bandile clenched his fists.

"What's your name, boy?"

"What's my name got to do with this?"

Bandile sighed and nodded, shrugging his shoulders.

"Nothing, I suppose."

He reached his hand out and tightened his grip around Martin's throat.

41

Flattening his foot on the accelerator, Eddie ran the third red light in the last three minutes.

He checked his watch. Not sure why; time wouldn't help him, nor would it indicate whether he would make it back before it was too late. He just needed something to glance at. Somewhere to direct his attention.

Struggling with directions, he made it to a roundabout next to the estate the boy lived on and racked his brain, trying to remember which way to go.

Was it left? Right? Straight on?

Left. It was left, surely.

Yet he recognised the houses to the right.

As he slowed down to a complete stop, the car behind him honked his horn.

"Fuck off!" Eddie shouted into his rear-view mirror.

Right. It must be right.

He shot his car around the roundabout, skidding into the right turn and into the estate.

He was correct. The decrepit houses around him were the same decrepit houses he had gone past earlier.

He wasn't far. Just around the corner. It must be

just around the corner.

A lady crossed the street with her child without looking and Eddie screeched to a halt. Gesturing his hands in the air to ask what the hell she was doing, she just squinted a repulsed look at him and continued.

He turned the corner and recognised the house beside him. Pulling the car to the side, halting it half over the pavement, half blocking someone's drive, he swung the car door open and dashed out.

Making his way around the car and skidding slightly, he ran up the narrow path to the house and banged on the door.

He banged again.

Nothing. No answer.

He tried the door handle. It was open.

Without giving it a second thought, he jumped over the threshold and through the doorway.

Rebounding off the side of the door, he ran into the living room and fell to his knees.

In front of him lay a vacant wheelchair on its side, the wheel still rotating slowly. Beside it, Martin lay upon the floor, groggy, blood trickling down his face and hoarse breathing exuding from his mouth.

He didn't need to search the house. Not this time. He knew she wouldn't be there.

They had her.

His fists clenched and he rose his head to the heavens, screaming out to the sky, putting all his anger and frustration into a bellow that made his throat sore.

If there is a God – something that, despite all he had done, he still occasionally doubted – *then why won't you lend us a hand?! Do something divine, intervene to help us! We fight your battle and you just sit there on your cloud and do nothing!*

They had everything they needed. The prophet, Bandile. The wounded, Anna. The suffered for a sacrifice, Kelly.

They also required 'the dead' – something Eddie had no idea where to search for, but ultimately, deep down, he knew they would have it.

They could now bring forth ·the devil. They could kill his girlfriend.

They could bring the heir of hell out of him.

And Eddie could do nothing about it.

He crawled forward toward Martin and turned him over. His eyes were open, but they were groggy, dizzy and suffering. He wept, but could force out no tears.

Eddie helped Martin onto the sofa, where he propped him up. He shook him slightly, knowing it would hurt him, but would have no choice.

"Martin, can you hear me?"

Martin blinked wearily and lifted his head.

"Martin, please, you have to answer me."

"Wh –" Martin coughed.

"Just give me an indication, Martin. Do they have her?"

Martin's eyebrows narrowed.

"Your mother. Do they have her?"

Eddie was able to detect a faint nod.

Fuck.

"And… who? Who did it?"

"Band… Bandi…" he attempted.

Eddie nodded. He didn't need to complete the name.

"Martin, do you have any idea where they took her? Any idea at all? Anything they said or did that might give us a clue?"

Martin's head dropped and shook back and forth.

"Okay," Eddie nodded.

He tried to find some words of comfort. Something he could say to him to indicate that his mum was safe.

He found himself at a loss.

Instead, he fetched him a wet towel and put it in his hand.

"Use this to dab your face. You'll be fine."

He wouldn't be fine. No one would. Soon, everyone would likely be dead.

42

Eddie stumbled onto the driveway and fell to his knees. The summer sun had gone and violent rain pounded downwards, hitting his face like liquid bullets.

He looked to the sky, his fists clenched, baring his teeth and moulding his mouth into a vehement scream.

A familiar presence came over him. Something he had not felt for years. Something that reminded him of the scorching heat of hell.

"Come on then," he sputtered antagonistically.

He looked around himself. Wind grew, bustling the hedges with more vigour, aggressively beating against Eddie's body.

"Come on then!" he rose his voice even louder.

The rain turned to sleet and he felt it shatter his face, but he did not falter. He turned his gaze to the sky and clenched his teeth.

"I know you are there! Come out and face me!"

"Okay, you can stop shouting."

His face jolted, turning immediately to the sound of the voice. The source of which stood in front of him with irritating arrogance.

A young girl, no more than seven or eight. Smiling. Feeling nothing of the torrential weather against her neat hair and black dress.

A bow even rested in her hair, a sweet smile planted on her smug head.

Eddie was not fooled.

"You are not the devil," Eddie grunted.

"No," the girl acknowledged with her sweet, unrelenting, playful tone. "He is busy. I am his messenger."

"He sent you?"

"This is a big night for him, as I'm sure you understand."

So it will be tonight... Eddie acknowledged.

"How have you done this? How have you put all of this into action?"

"It was simple, really," the girl boasted. "All we needed was your idiocy and foolishness to play on."

Eddie's knees grew sore digging into the rough cement beneath him, his nails dug into his palms and his teeth grinded. But the idea that he had been tricked into this line of events hurt more than anything.

"I don't believe you."

"Honestly, when you came down to hell to save Derek's soul and you were able to escape – did you really think it would be that easy?"

"I won that battle, fair and square."

The girl burst out laughing. "You think you won against the devil? Please." Her laughing ceased and expression deadened. "He let you go."

"Why?"

"Because he needed you to fall in love with Kelly. He needed you to keep the one who had suffered close, so that when the time was right, she would be with you. Close to you."

Close to me? They are doing the ceremony close to me?

"I get it, because I have a piece of evil somewhere in me and you needed me for it."

"It is more than just a piece of evil now, Edward. You have the devil inside of you."

"Oh, shut up, I have heard this enough."

"No, you don't understand. When you came down to hell to fight for Derek's soul, he let you escape. When he did this, he latched a piece of himself onto your soul. He did this the same way Lamashtu did when you crossed over for the first time as a very young child. And ever since that night, he has been driving you."

"Driving me?"

"Yes. You may have been the vehicle, but he has been behind the steering wheel."

It hit him. Flashes of his memory, winding around his mind like a tornado. Pinning the cat to the wall of the shed, the Latin writing, the carcasses strewn around his house... it was him. He had done every bit of it.

Except, it wasn't him. It was his hands, yes, but he had played no part.

But it all made sense. If the devil had a piece of him inside, he wouldn't want Eddie to know. He would need to keep it secret. So he could bring all this to happen.

"So why would you tell me this? Why would the devil send you, so I would know that the ritual would be at my house?"

"Because he needs you there. For the ritual, he needs you there. It would succeed without you, but it would be a far slower process."

"Then how does he know I will show? Maybe I'll get a plane ticket, get as far away as I can."

She giggled. "Because he has the one you love. Kelly. And he will kill her, with you there or not. And he knows you would not resist trying to stop it."

She was right. He loathed himself for it, but she was right.

The whole world would not end if he left, but Kelly – she would die. A thought that was unbearable.

Is this selfish? Should I just let her…

But the thought didn't even finish in his mind.

"Isn't he afraid I will stop it? Now I know all this?"

"The devil sent me as a courtesy, because he wishes you to know. If there was anything you could do I wouldn't be here. It is hopeless. It will all come to be."

"But I could stop him. I *will* stop him."

"Edward, you don't understand. You have no power against him. You are his son."

"I am not his son."

"By the end of the night, you will be. Once the ritual is complete, that piece inside of you that gives you your powers, the piece the devil has planted a part of him inside you, it will have grown. It will have consumed you. You will no longer be Edward King. You will be his son and you will do his bidding."

"No I won't."

"These events have been put into place since you faced Balam on Millennium Night. There is nothing you can do to stop it now. Resistance is futile, you must understand. To fight will only cause more pain."

He bowed his head. His hair was drenched to his

scalp, in pain from the beating of the sleet, shaking from the cold of the torrential wind. He felt sick. He wanted to fight, he wanted to do everything he could, but in his gut he knew the truth.

It was over.

"Take me…" he muttered.

"Pardon?" the girl smiled, bemused.

Eddie rose his head and locked eyes with her.

"Take me. The devil can have me. I'll fulfil the prophecy. I'll do it all. Take me now. Just spare Kelly. Spare her and I won't resist."

The girl stepped forward and planted a gentle hand on the side of his face. She crouched down before him, stroking her fingers on the underside of his chin and smiling a lost smile.

"If you had given us that offer a year ago, we would have taken it."

"What?" Eddie faltered.

"But The Devil's Three is ready. The ritual is inevitable."

"But you can have me!"

"You don't see it, Edward." She leant toward him and whispered in a deep voice that did not match the young, sweet face before him. "Why would the devil have something, when he could have everything?" Leaving those words echoing in the air, she disappeared into darkness and was gone.

Eddie was left on his knees, crying tears into rain.

All he could do now was fight. Fight, despite it meaning nothing.

43

25 July 2002

The clocked ticked past midnight as Jenny turned and sighed with exasperation.

Three hours she had been lying there, urging herself to sleep. She didn't know what it was that was making her so restless, but her insomnia was making her more and more aggravated; which, in turn, made her all the less likely to be able to sleep.

Something inside her was niggling away. A bad feeling, like something awful was about to happen, keeping her awake.

Beside her, Lacy lay silently, breathing deeply. She was so beautiful, and Jenny couldn't help but smile. Lacy was on her side, turned toward Jenny, with her hand draped affectionately over Jenny's torso.

Jenny wondered what she was dreaming about, if she was dreaming at all. She loved her so much.

Deciding she could not stand just lying there, driving herself mad, getting frustrated that she couldn't shut off her mind, she sat up in bed. Running her hands over her head and through her hair, she paused for a moment, then grabbed her glass and left the room.

She crept downstairs – Lacy didn't need waking up because she couldn't sleep – and tiptoed across to the kitchen.

Her bare feet felt cold on the tiled floor and it took her a moment to adjust. She kept the light off, using the hazy illumination from the moon outside the window to guide her way to the fridge. Opening the fridge, she withdrew a carton of milk and poured it into her glass.

She leant against the sink, motionless, cradling the glass in her hand. Out the window, the weather was attacking their garden. Rain pelted down like a meteor shower, wind throwing the leaves on the trees to the side and thunder echoing in the distance.

It was like the weather was somehow mirroring her uncertainty. Whatever was keeping her awake, she couldn't figure it out.

Then, almost as if answering her question, the phone rang. With a glance at the clock, she wondered who would be ringing at this time.

She picked up the receiver and held it to her ear, flinching at first as it felt cold.

"Hello?"

Silence. The line crackled and spewed discordance.

"Hello?" she prompted again.

"… Jenny," came a feeble voice.

She recognised her best friend's voice straight away.

"Eddie?"

"… Jenny … I …" he stuttered.

"Eddie, is everything okay?"

Eddie didn't reply. She could almost hear him thinking, mulling over issues sitting prominently in his mind.

The faint sound of sobbing mixed with the cracking of the line.

"Eddie, what is going on?"

"Jenny, you… you've been my best friend my whole life."

"I have. What's going on?"

"I just wanted to say…"

He trailed off into static. Jenny's arms shook. Something was wrong.

"Eddie, please tell me what is going on?"

"I just wanted to tell you, whatever happens… I love you. And I'm grateful for all you've done."

"Eddie, what –"

She had no time to ask the question before the line went dead and she was presented with the numbing sound of the dial tone.

Something was wrong. He sounded practically dead. His voice was despondent, reluctant.

The bad feeling in her gut keeping her awake miraculously explained itself.

In a burst of energy, she ran up the stairs, stomping on each step in hope of waking Lacy, and burst into the bedroom.

"Lacy, wake up." She shoved her partner.

"What?" Lacy fumbled, her eyes fluttering hazily.

"You need to get up, something's wrong with Eddie."

"Huh?" Lacy leant up and looked around the room, looking at the clock and sighing. "What is going on?"

"It's Eddie," Jenny answered, her serious tone

sending chills through Lacy and waking her instantly. "We need to go."

Jenny changed into a t-shirt and jeans within seconds, dumping her pyjamas on the floor and shoving a pile of clothes at Lacy.

"What's happened to him?" Lacy stuttered, climbing out of bed without full awareness of what her tired mind was doing.

"Lacy, please hurry up."

Jenny's eyes filled with tears and she didn't need to say another word to show Lacy she was serious.

44

Eddie's watch read 2.32 a.m.

His palms were sweaty. A sickening feeling spewed around his stomach. His legs were jelly, wobbling and buckling under the pressure.

The weather hit him with a ferocious punch, rain and sleet battering against him, scolding his face. Dark clouds loomed above, thunder rang out and lightening seized a blinding flash in the distance.

Before him stood his house. The home he and Kelly had made for themselves. The place they had paid a deposit for with joyous optimism and passion for each other. A place full of photographs displaying memories. A place warmed by heating and love. A place where they had truly fallen in love.

A place that would be the setting of the coming of the antichrist.

There was nothing more he could do now but fight. Fight what, he didn't know; but whatever came, he would put up a barricade and resist with everything he had.

His powers could become useless, his detriment could fall and his integrity could be destroyed.

But as long as he could, he would stand between this world and the one that claimed he was Eddie's true father.

Yet, as he stood there preparing his resistance,

willing strength to his heart and protection to his soul, he found himself twitching.

His fingers at first, then the pain seized up through his arm and triggered his elbows to flinch.

His heart thumped and he felt his legs overcome, his face stiffen and frozen ice seep through him like cyanide.

He was not in control.

That thing inside of him, those powers, this 'gift' – it spread into his bones, into his muscles, consuming his blood.

That thing he felt inside of him, that resistance he could access when fighting any demon, grew stronger. It felt like a happy illness. It shook his body. It took him over.

He willed his feet not to move but they moved nonetheless.

He rigidly stepped forward with straightened legs. Feeling like a piece of artificial intelligence, sitting in the backseat of his mind, he lifted his hand forward and unlocked the front door to his house.

He crossed the threshold, intentionally leaving the door open.

He cried, but nothing came out. His tears were blanks firing out of a broken cannon. He felt his muscles move, his bones twinge, but he was doing none of it.

"Edward…" came the whispers of his mind.

Opening a drawer in the kitchen, he found a large piece of rope, ankle restraints, and handcuffs.

How the fuck did they get there…

He had never owned such things, never mind had them to hand in a kitchen drawer he accessed most days.

Then he remembered.

He had put them there.

Except, he hadn't. His hands had, but his mind had been absent.

The image came around in a flash. His hands below him placing the rope in, barely visible through the pitch-black of night.

Everything the devil had planned had come to pass.

With his spare arm, he took a wooden chair from the kitchen and carried it into the living room. A more open space was needed. The living room would be the perfect setting.

We can do it here.

He sat on the chair, pausing for a moment, his eyes deadened on the door before him. The draft from the front door was reaching around the hallway and grabbing him.

He shook. Through fear, cold, or simply being out of control of his own body, he did not know.

He mechanically reached his hands down with robotic perfection. He lifted the ankle restraints in his hand. He placed one metallic circle around his left ankle, looped the chain behind the chair legs and fastened his right ankle in.

Tightening them until they were painfully constricted, he turned the key in the lock. He lifted the key in his hands and threw it out of the room.

Nothing made sense. Gut full of hatred, heart full of malice, he felt anger exuding out of him.

He was turning. The ritual hadn't even started yet and already he was on his way.

He placed the handcuffs around his wrists and looped them through the back of the chair. The key flew into the air of its own accord and disappeared around the corner of the hallway.

He was secure.

With an abrupt wave of euphoria that felt like someone had thrown a bucket of cold water over him, he came around.

His consciousness came to. He felt himself again. He was in control.

Except, he couldn't move. He banged his ankles side to side and pulled at his handcuffs. They were wrapped around his bones in a painful grip and he wasn't going anywhere.

The sound of the front door slamming shut coincided with a strike of lightning. Faint voices grew louder and footsteps approached.

Bandile appeared around the corner, wearing that same grin.

That same fucking grin.

Eddie's eyes narrowed, and every bit of anger reached his face, directed at the bastard in front of him.

"Hello, Eddie," Bandile greeted him.

Picking up the rope Eddie had left beside his feet, Bandile tied it around Eddie's torso repeatedly until all of Eddie's movement was completely constricted.

Eddie looked Bandile in the eyes.

"If I ever get out of this," Eddie spat, "I will kill you, you sick fucking bastard."

"Edward," Bandile replied soothingly. "You will not be getting out of this."

Tightening the last knot of the rope, Bandile stood, shouting around the corner, "We're ready!"

Anna appeared first. Floating. Levitating through the air, across the room. Her face was a veiny mess, blue and grey, with scabs peeling off.

She fell to the ground behind Eddie.

Next appeared a man Eddie barely recognised at first, then recoiled in horror to see.

Jason Aslan. The man whose head had been removed in front of him.

"How the…" Eddie stuttered.

His question didn't last long as his heart filled with pain. Jason's hand gripped over the hair of Kelly.

She too was in ankle restraints, handcuffs, and rope, unable to move, completely immobile. Being dragged across the room by Jason, a fistful of hair in his hand, Kelly's hoarse voice barely able to scream out in terror any longer.

Eddie cried. It was all he could do. Weeping tears of anger down his face.

He couldn't move. He couldn't do a damn thing to help her. He was useless.

She couldn't even look at him.

Jason dumped her beside Eddie's feet and took his position next to Eddie.

Bandile collected a bin bag from the side of the door and poured the contents over Kelly. Numerous dead animals, gutted, slit, ripped apart, fell over her.

She gagged and threw up. The stench was unbearable. The blood fell off them and dripped down Kelly's chin.

Bandile took his place, completing the triangle surrounding Eddie and Kelly.

"Are we ready?" he asked.

Jason nodded.

Anna nodded.

"Excellent," he confirmed.

He grinned at Eddie.

"Then we shall begin."

45

"*Diabolus enim accersam te,*" Bandile whispered in a low, hushed voice. "*Diabolus enim accersam te. Diabolus enim accersam te.*"

Eddie didn't know Latin well. But he recognised those words. He had come across the words 'devil' and 'summon' enough to understand when they were being spoken.

"You don't have to do this," Eddie announced.

"*Diabolus enim accersam te. Diabolus enim accersam te.*"

"Whatever the devil has offered you, it isn't worth it," Eddie assured.

"Devil, please take this offering. Please grant us your presence, tell us we are worthy."

Bandile grabbed Kelly by the hair and lifted her up.

"No, please, don't!" Eddie cried out.

Bandile snarled at Eddie.

"Don't fucking touch her!" he screamed over the sound of the rain thrashing the windows.

"Devil, please help us silence him," Bandile spoke, looking Eddie straight in the eyes.

A slash of blood appeared over Eddie's face, stinging him with agony. It felt like a knife had pierced his skin and it did nothing but strengthen his resolve.

"I pray thee, those gathered in The Devil's Three, please. Continue our prayer."

Jason and Anna did as they were instructed, chanting repeatedly, "D*iabolus enim accersam te, diabolus enim accersam te.*"

Bandile withdrew a grand knife from the back of his waist band. The handle of the knife was brown leather, with spaces for fingers to grip. The blade was like a stretched-out claw, bumps in the inside and a sharp, fierce curve on the outside.

He put the knife next to Kelly's throat.

Kelly locked eyest with Eddie. For the first time since she had entered the room, she looked him in the eyes. She had resisted up until now, but in that moment, facing the final seconds of her life, she couldn't help but look into the eyes of the man she loved.

"Eddie…please…"

He willed his powers to do something. His gift to reveal. Conjure a fireball, rip out the demon, throw some piece of wind forward and throw the bastard with a knife next to her throat flat out against the far wall.

But nothing happened. And Bandile's prayer continued.

"We sacrifice this, the suffered. Suffered by your hands. We hope you take it."

Kelly's eyes faded. Her mouth quivered into a tearful, hopeless mess.

Eddie saw the woman he loved and everything he loved about her.

The moment he first met her. In the hospital. They shared the awful hospital dinners. They discussed their life philosophies.

He never left. By her side, he had stayed for days.

Their first date. She got ice cream down her face. He laughed. He said he'd get rid of it for her. He kissed her.

Their first kiss. Her lips had been so soft. She tasted like chocolate flake. They had paused in that moment for so long.

When he had told her he loved her. She said she had been waiting for him to say that for so long so she could say it too.

"Edward King. It is time to embrace your destiny."

Kelly's eyes closed. Her face scrunched up. She begged for her life.

"Once the suffered is dead, your true form will rise."

"I love you, Kelly," he whispered.

She didn't answer. Her eyes were tightened close, her face scrunched up, preparing herself for the impact of the knife.

"It is going to happen."

Bandile retracted the knife back, pulling it, preparing to lunge it forward.

"Not if I have something to say about it," announced a voice from the far side of the room.

Kelly's eyes opened with a start. Eddie's jaw dropped. Bandile's head shot around.

"Let the girl go," demanded Derek.

46

Derek was thrashing, kicking, and punching, doing whatever he could.

Until he couldn't.

His body went limp.

That's when he saw it. A bright, shining, white light.

Was this it? Was this the end?

A hand reached down, grabbing hold of his arm. He felt it being pulled. A very loose acknowledgement of something happening crossed his mind.

Then it went blank.

When he opened his eyes, he was on his back, on a surface of hard sand. He coughed, spewing water out of his lungs, turning onto his side.

He tried leaning up, but couldn't. His arms were motionless. His body too weak.

He was alive. He knew he was alive. But barely.

"Derek."

A woman's voice echoed in his mind.

He saw nothing.

The amber glow above him was out of focus, the light-blue sky a hazy blur. He could smell sea. He could feel sand trickling between his fingers. He could even taste the clean air.

But his vision did not return.

"Derek."

He heard it once more.

"Look at me, Derek."

A soothing, sweet female voice rang out. It sounded like it was in his mind. A hallucination. A mirage, maybe.

"Look up, Derek, you can see me."

A bright, blurred light covered his vision. Slowly but steadily, it came into focus, and Derek could see before him.

"What?" he muttered.

"You're okay, Derek," this woman's voice told him. "You're going to survive."

Squinting, readjusting his eyes, shaking his head to allow him to see, he finally laid his eyes on the beauty before him.

A woman, with long, blond, flowing hair and a white dress that glided off her body, floated in the air. From behind her came a blinding-white light, so bright her faultless, smooth face was barely visible.

She illuminated over him. An angel. A gift from the gods.

"Who are you?" Derek managed, still coughing up water.

"My name is Cassy," the heavenly voice announced. "We have never met."

"Cassy?"

"I am Eddie's younger sister. I died when he was

young. Eddie freed me."

Derek's mind came into focus. His ringing ears diluted to clarity, the strength returning to his muscles. He leant up, propping himself up on his elbows, and cast his eyes over the floating spirit.

"You're dead."

"It's true, I died. But when I died I was given an option. Go on to heaven, or return and help save Eddie and the world from the fate of hell."

"What?"

"You need to listen carefully to me, Derek. Jason Aslan returned in the devil's name and sent your plane crashing and you to a certain death. Now heaven has played its part. They sent me. To save you."

Derek sat in awe, speechless.

"But I come with bad news."

"What?"

"You have six days to return home."

"Why? What happens then?"

"Bandile Thato and Jason Aslan have been tasked with assisting the devil in his ascension. They are determined to summon and unleash the antichrist within Eddie."

"What? Jason Aslan? He's dead."

Cassy remained silent. Derek slowly appreciated that maybe there was more going on than he could be completely aware of.

"How do you know this?" he demanded.

She looked away from him for a moment. He thought he could see the sadness in her expression.

"It is my job to know," she told him. But Derek knew there was more to the story. Beatific angel, hallucination, or ghost; she was not telling him the whole truth.

"I was sent back to intervene on this day. And I will intervene. I will come, I will do my part. But I can only provide humanity with the tools; heaven cannot intervene with free will. That is where I need you."

Derek looked around himself. He was on an island. A piece of desert surrounded by water.

"Where am I?"

"Somewhere in the Andaman Sea. South of the Andaman and Nicobar Islands."

"What?"

"Go north up the sea, to a place called Rutland Island. You will find transport there."

"How do I…?"

"Good luck, Derek. Please. Save my brother."

She faded, her bright luminosity dissolving into absence of matter. Around him was nothing but emptiness.

No other survivors were on the island. He was alone.

Getting to his feet, he peered across the sea. Sure enough, in the distance, he could see the outline of another island. There was movement he couldn't make out.

But there was movement nonetheless. This meant there was life.

He approached the sea. His muscles felt full of vitality, which was peculiar, considering they were immovable only moments before.

He knew what he had seen. What he had been told.

Cassy had given him a helping hand.

Finally, they were not fighting this fight alone.

He dove into the sea and swam. It took him only eighteen minutes until he reached the Port of Rutland Island.

The first thing he did was find a map, indicating where he was. A small island. Next to Thailand, south of Myanmar. East of Sri Lanka.

Southeast of India.

That was his starting point. He could take a boat from the port and use it to get to India. From there, he could travel across Pakistan, risk his way through Iran and Iraq, cross into Turkey. Then he would be in Europe. From there, he could make his way across Bulgaria, Czech Republic, Germany, to France. He could make his way to the Channel Tunnel.

It was doable.

The only question was whether he would make it in six days.

It was too long to go to be able to reach England by then. Then another reality check occurred to him; he had no passport. No money. How was he supposed to get across any borders or find any transport with that?

"Excuse me?" came a voice from behind him. Derek spun around and saw a short, thin Indian man. "Is your name Derek?"

Derek nodded absentmindedly, still focussed on his travels.

"My name is Ahmed. This is hard to explain, but…"

Derek turned his body fully toward him. "You saw her too?" he asked.

"Yes… I did," Ahmed nodded.

"And what did she tell you?"

"She said there was a man called Derek, who

needed my help. That the world may depend on it. And it was my choice to intervene."

Derek stepped toward him. "And are you able to help?"

"I have a boat," the man offered weakly. "It's not big, but it will get you across the ocean. It will take a while, but –"

"How long is a while?"

"Six days, maybe," Ahmed shrugged.

Derek put his hand on Ahmed's shoulder and nodded. He had no time to lose.

47

As she glanced at the dashboard clock and saw 2.58 a.m., Jenny couldn't believe how awake she actually was. Lacy sat faithfully in the passenger seat beside her, but her head was dropping and she was dozing. Her urgency obviously hadn't paid off.

All she cared about was getting to Eddie's house before he did anything stupid.

What could it be? Could he have reverted back to the Eddie from around six or seven years ago? The Eddie who tried to kill himself?

He had come so far, achieved so much, it would be hard to envisage his strong personality dropping so much as an inch these days. He had, quite literally, taken on hell itself.

So why was it that phone call terrified her so much?

"I wanted to tell you I love you."

"Thank you for all you have done."

The words rang in her head like the crash of a cymbal that wouldn't stop shaking. Those words did not sound hopeful – those words sounded like goodbye.

Like he was preparing to do something drastic.

Jenny meandered the car into the fast lane of the motorway and started stewing at the ridiculously slow driver in front. She was fully aware she was speeding excessively, but there was a middle lane free beside her, why wasn't this idiot moving into it?

After she rode their bumper, the car finally moved over. Ignoring the middle finger that went up at her as she overtook, she remained focussed on the task ahead.

"Slow down, sweetheart," Lacy requested, her eyes opening quickly as she became more aware of Jenny's driving.

"I can't."

"We want to get there in one piece, don't we?"

Lacy placed an affectionate hand on Jenny's leg. She was right. Crashing would be no good to anyone.

But Lacy hadn't heard the phone call.

She wasn't aware of the reason behind the panic.

Swinging into the slip road, she accelerated the car toward the roundabout and broke suddenly as a car came to her right. Shifting into second gear, she sped up quickly, ignoring the strenuous sound of the strained engine and zooming onto the A road.

"What did Eddie say?" Lacy enquired, keen to know why Jenny was driving so recklessly.

"He said… he said goodbye."

Her heart sank.

Lacy nodded in understanding.

Shooting past a speed camera, not caring about the white flash, Jenny turned into an estate and spun around the corner down Eddie's road.

It was as if the weather got even worse as they

entered the road. The tyres skidded over the icy, wet surface and the windscreen wipers could barely keep the rain off the car long enough for Jenny to be able to see.

Eddie's curtains were drawn.

She screeched the car to a halt, pulled on the handbrake and sprinted out of the car, Lacy following.

By the time they got to the front door, they were drenched. The space of twelve yards down the driveway was enough to drown them.

Jenny thumped her fist against the door.

"Eddie! Eddie, open up!"

The door opened. A man in his fifties answered, looking calmly back at her.

"Where's Eddie?" Jenny demanded. "Who are you?"

"My name is Jason," replied the man. "It's so lovely for you to join us."

48

Eddie's mind was full of fear. Terrified, wide eyes stared at Kelly struggling on the floor, her whole body bound, attempting to wriggle away. Terrified for his own safety, what he was becoming. Terrified for what mankind was about to face.

Yet, before him, was his mentor. Derek appeared tired, worn-out, downtrodden, but resilient. Determined. Chastised but adamant he would not be defeated. His strength was overwhelming.

Bandile, however, was not one to give in easily.

He charged forward, stepping over the dead animals laid over the floor, putting his hand around Derek's throat and shoving him against the wall.

"You said he was dead!" Bandile bellowed at Jason.

Four loud thumps resounded from the front door.

"Get it," Bandile sneered at Jason, baring his teeth. "And deal with whoever it is."

Jason bundled out of the room with his head down, ashamed, saddened. He had failed his part of the mission.

Derek did all he could to fight against Bandile, but Bandile's muscles were large and his will was strong.

Derek flailed his hands out, punching Bandile in the gut, in the face, anywhere he could reach. But

Bandile's hand around Derek's neck was suffocating him so much he couldn't even choke. He could feel the walls of his throat closing in, pressing toward his oesophagus.

With a quick surge of strength, Derek flung his arms upwards and landed them into Bandile's elbow, momentarily knocking his hand away from his throat. Bandile did not falter for long, punching Derek in the face and throwing him to the floor by the neck.

Eddie turned his head toward Kelly. She was creeping away toward the door, slowly but determinedly, desperate to lurch herself out. The rope around her body was fraying and he could see rashes on her bare arms, and her ankles were restricting her legs quite severely.

Anna sprung forward from behind Eddie and pounced upon Kelly. Anna's legs were unusable, her body crippled and exhausted, but her torso had enough gusto to hold Kelly down.

Bandile's knife lay an arm stretch away from Anna.

Derek freed himself of Bandile's gasp and dove forward onto Anna, reaching out for the knife until –

"*Stop!*" cried out Jason.

Everyone froze.

He stood in the doorway, a knife in each of his hands, Jenny and Lacy cowering in front of him.

Each knife was pressed against their neck.

"Derek," Jason panted, out of breath. "Back away from the girl, or they will die."

"No."

"Derek..." Eddie whimpered.

His friends. His girlfriend. Everything he had to lose sat poised on a knife edge before him.

"Eddie, come to your senses," Derek furiously whispered. "If they finish the ceremony it will be done, no return. You will be gone. We have to make sacrifices."

Eddie looked from Derek's pleading eyes to Bandile, who returned the stare from his knees, pressurising Derek's legs.

Eddie looked to Jason, whose eyes were going, a man at the end of his tether. Hopeless. Desperate.

Then Eddie looked to Jenny and Lacy. Their eyes full of distress. He had brought them here. That stupid phone call had brought them here.

Finally, he glanced at Kelly. The woman he loved. Bound, humiliated, at the end of her life. Laying beneath Anna, who held the curved blade high above her head.

Eddie's eyes met Derek's once more.

"No, Derek, I'm sorry," he sobbed, his eyes full of tears. "There are some sacrifices I cannot make."

"The fate of the world depends on this, Eddie."

Eddie shook his head. He couldn't. As much as he knew Derek was talking sense, as much as he knew he was right, he couldn't. He rose his head to Jason.

"Let them go."

Anna took the opportunity without hesitation.

She lifted the knife into the air and brought it down with shuddering speed toward Kelly's gut.

49

Anna froze.

Her knife halted a foot above Kelly.

She was motionless.

As was Kelly, who was stuck in a wide-mouth gape of horror.

In fact, everyone but Eddie was frozen still in their fixed position. Derek staring back at him with feeble eyes, Jason's knives pushing against Jenny's and Lacy's throats, Bandile lying upon Derek's legs.

The scene had turned to a black-and-white, motionless still image. Whether it was his sight, his mind, his stress, he did not know. Nothing moved.

Then, as if answering his question, the reason approached Eddie from behind.

"Beautiful, isn't it?" came the voice of the little girl he had seen earlier that night.

She made her way around Eddie's body and sat on his lap, tormenting him with her pretty, virginal appearance. Mocking the powers he fought for with her pure, white dress.

"Get the fuck off me," Eddie growled.

"Ooh," the girl retracted playfully. "That's not very nice."

The girl patted Eddie on his head and skipped over to Kelly. She crouched down beside her.

Kelly's face was stuck in an image of pure horror. Her eyes displaying sheer agony, staring rigidly at the knife about to plunge through her.

"Cute, ain't she?" smiled the girl. "Can see why you picked her."

Eddie's eyes narrowed, his face shook, his fists clenched. He wished he could storm forward and rip this girl's throat out. He wished he could end her pitiful, tormenting appearance once and for all.

"Wow," the girl shook her head in disbelief. "I can feel the hate coming off you. The anger, the hostility, it's already there. You are on your way."

"Let me out of these restraints and we'll see who's on our way."

"Now, now, all in good time."

The little girl stood and inquisitively surveyed Eddie.

"You do by now realise, surely, that we have won."

"Fuck you."

"Yes, protest all you wish. The ritual has been completed, the girl is about to be stabbed, it is complete."

"No, it isn't. The suffered has to die. Kelly is getting stabbed in the gut, there's no way to know she is dead."

"I know. That's where you come in."

The girl skipped over to the sofa and plopped herself down. She picked up a television paper left on the seat beside her, remanents of the normal life Eddie was leading only days ago. She flicked through it playfully, not staying on one page too long.

"My, my, look at all these soap operas," she smiled, shaking her head in pretend disgust. "All the violence, shooting, cheating. To think, all this goes on in your world, and you need it for entertainment. Honestly, Edward. I think the world will be better off."

"What do you want from me?"

"I want you to kill Kelly."

Eddie laughed defiantly, vigorously shaking his head.

"You've got to be kidding. Why would I do that?"

"Because, Edward," she stood and turned serious, "We have already won. The ritual is on its way. And you killing Kelly will be your final task into ascension. And, as fate would have it, it is the only way to save your friends."

"Save them by killing them?"

"Exactly."

She walked over to Anna and peeled back the fingers that grasped the knife, peeling it out of her hand. She pushed Anna back and Anna flopped onto the floor without straying from her stiff, stationary position.

The girl marvelled at the knife in her hands.

"I need you to take this knife," she instructed Eddie. "And stick it in the throat of your girlfriend."

"Why would I do that?"

"Because the ritual is already done. She is going to die."

The girl approached Eddie and put her hand on Eddie's shoulder, looking him dead in his fuming eyes.

"If you don't do it, I will click my fingers and everyone here will fall down dead. Derek. Lacy. Jenny. They will all just drop to the floor and cease breathing. And Kelly here, who is already on her way, will suffer in hell forever."

She stroked her hand down Eddie's face and smiled.

"If you do it, however – we will spare your friend's their imminent death. And we will allow Kelly's soul to pass on to heaven, where she will avoid an eternity of suffering."

She placed the knife on Eddie's lap.

"The choice is yours."

With a final glistening of her eyes, her body faded and she was gone.

Eddie looked down. The rope, the handcuffs, the ankle restraints – they had all disappeared too. He was free.

He took the knife in his palm. Turned it over in his hands. Looked at the blood of Kelly dripping off it.

His eyes rose. His friends were still immobile, stuck in a moment of terror. Kelly still lay on the floor in horror. His friends still stood staring at him hopelessly.

This was it. Refuse and they all dropped down dead. Kelly would be tortured forever.

Do it and they would be free. Kelly would be given passage to heaven.

But that would mean truly accepting his fate.

Tears trickled down his cheek. He knew what he had to do.

He stood. His knees felt weak, collapsing beneath him, but he stayed strong. Kept his posture up. Took a few definite strides toward the one he would do anything for.

The one he would die for.

The one he would *kill* for.

He knelt down beside her. Brushing his hand down

her face, he shut her eyes and pushed her jaw up to allow her lips to meet. The look of horror was gone. She was peaceful.

One moment and she would be forever peaceful.

He could already feel the change. Feel the power surging through him, feel himself detesting the humanity of the world. Feeling his loyalties shift to that of hell. Of the devil.

Of his father.

He lifted the knife in the air and screamed as he plunged it downward, into the throat of the suffered.

50

Derek recoiled in shock. He couldn't believe what he was seeing. He didn't know how Eddie had freed himself from his restraints, how he had gotten himself to Kelly's side, but most of all he couldn't believe what Eddie was doing.

Eddie retracted the knife from Kelly's throat and a puddle of blood gushed beneath her neck. She looked up at Eddie, her eyes weak.

Her stare focussed on Eddie's.

Her eyes were lost. Fading as they stared up at the man she had given her heart to as he murdered her. She suffocated for mere moments before she passed out.

The last thing she saw before she died was the face of her killer.

The face of the man she trusted.

Eddie looked up and met Derek's eyes.

Derek shook his head in disbelief. In disgust.

"How could you..." he cried, his strong façade faltering to fatigue.

"It was the only way," Eddie replied.

Then he was Eddie no more.

Eddie cried out in pain as his skin stretched over him, ripping. It shedded like snake skin, peeling and floating into ashes, bringing forth a creature unrecognisable from the human Eddie had previously been.

His pupils turned red, his hands turned to claws.

A monster forced its way out, claws of animalistic torture hanging off him, snarling drool dripping from his fangs.

Derek fell back, his heart thumping like a seizing drum, helplessly crying.

Bandile and Jason fell to their knees in honour, bowing their heads.

Jenny and Lacy backed up against the wall, keeping themselves far away.

Eddie King now had dark, blood-red skin, veins prominently pronounced over the entirety of his body, his nails curved and his body lurching over the rest of the room.

Horns grew from his head and curved into an impending shadow.

Behind him appeared another red, horned figure. A figure of similar appearance, but far more aged, far more aware of its existence.

The two creatures stood loyally together. In a clash of lightning, a pounding of thunder and a trickle of flames, they were gone.

Eddie King was gone.

The creature he had become had left the ritual with a final, carnivorous growl.

In the room of loss that remained, Jason's body faded to white and floated upwards, travelling, ascending on its resolution.

Bandile grabbed Anna and fled the room.

Jenny and Lacy wept. On the floor, clinging to each other, they whimpered and cried, drowned out by the rain beating against the window.

Derek remained on his knees, hopelessly muttering in despair. His eyes fixed on the spot his friend had been. A feeling of emptiness filled his stomach.

If you listened very carefully, you could just about make out the words he wept.

"I have failed you. I have failed you…"

But even those words faded.

The only element that did not cease was the weather.

In fact, if anything, the rain just grew stronger.

"You cannot drink the cup of the Lord and the cup of demons.

You cannot partake of the table of the Lord and the table of demons."

Corinthians 10:20-21

51

Martin lay inconsolably on the floor of his living room, strewn over the empty wheelchair, empty in the absence of its owner.

His bruises still hurt and the weather was still loud, but this was not the pain that stabbed him the harshest.

All the love he had given Ma, all the help he had given her, it had all turned to nothing. She was gone. And he didn't even understand why.

"Martin," came a gentle voice from behind him.

He slowly turned his head around and collapsed in awe.

A bright-white light illuminated the room, flooding from behind a beautiful woman in a pure, white dress. Her long, blond hair glided downwards and her smile captivated him.

As she floated before him, Martin could barely speak.

"Martin, my name is Cassy," she told him. "And I have come with a message."

"A message?" Martin repeated, confused.

His head pounded. So much had happened in such a small time, he couldn't quite believe his eyes.

What was this woman, and how was she so bright? How was she floating?

"What are you?" he demanded.

"I am an angel, Martin. I understand you may be shocked, but we don't have much time."

"Time for what?"

"The whole world rests on your shoulders."

The whole world? Resting on his shoulders? What?

I'm a school dropout. A friendless bum. A poor excuse for a man with no family and, soon, nowhere to live.

"I am not some brave man, I'm afraid. You have the wrong person."

"On the contrary, my boy. You are one of the bravest men to ever live. The love you have for your mother beams off you. To have that kind of love in the situation you have been in, it is divine."

"What?"

"And for that divine reason, the world needs you, Martin."

He bowed his head and shook it.

"Your mother needs you."

He closed his eyes. He couldn't do this. Not now. It was too much.

"Please, just leave me alone."

"Martin, I need you to be strong. As strong as you can be. For what I have to tell you is not going to be easy."

He lifted his head.

"What?" he grunted. "I'm not strong. I'm a loser. I'm worth shit. Go bother someone else."

The woman smiled.

"Martin, the man who visited you earlier was, in life, my brother. And right now he needs both our help. Right now, he needs everyone's help."

Martin sighed and looked around the room, willing her to leave him to grieve.

"And what do you want from me?"

"It's time for you to step up and fulfil the destiny you have been waiting for your whole life. It's time to save your mother's soul, and every other soul in the world."

"What?"

"Martin, I need you to kill my brother, Edward King."

Message from the author:

Thank you so much for not only reading my latest instalment in *The Edward King Series* – but for investing in these characters for three books.

I hope that, for fans of this series, this will really set you up nicely for the final two books. There are still plenty of twists and turns in store!

If you enjoyed it, then please consider writing me a customer review on Amazon. They make a huge difference to how well a book does, and each one is a huge bit of encouragement to me as I'm powering my way through writing them.

You can also join my Reader's Group and receive a free and exclusive prequel to *The Edward King Series*. Join at http://www.rickwoodwriter.com/sign-up

Thank you again for reading and for your terrific support.

All the best,
Rick

Join the Reader's Group at

www.rickwoodwriter.com

and get the FREE and EXCLUSIVE prequel to The Edward King Series

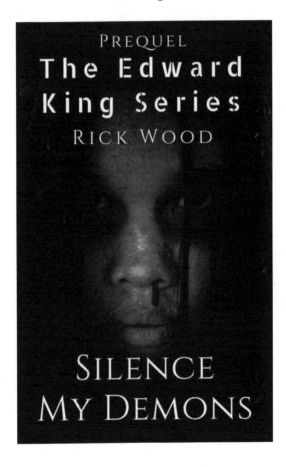

OUT NOW:

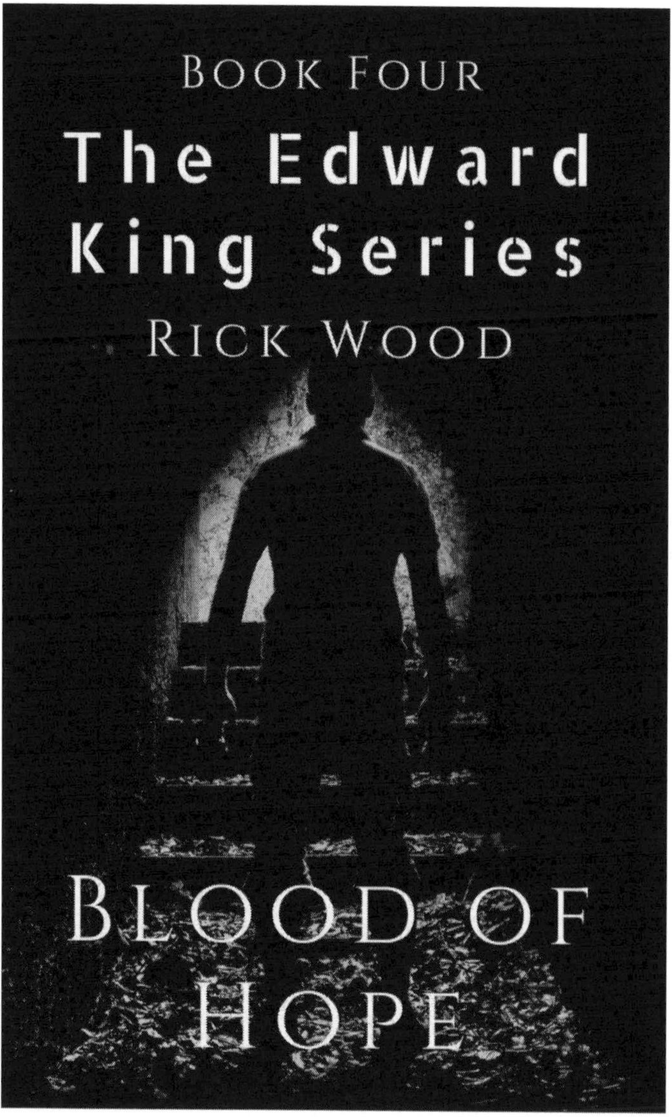

You can also like Rick Wood on Facebook: @rickwoodthewriter

You can follow Rick Wood on Twitter: @rickwoodwriter

And you can follow him on Instagram: @rickwoodwriter

10597627R00150

Printed in Great Britain
by Amazon